Andy Warhol's

KIM NEWMAN

Andy Warhol's Dracula

The right of Kim Newman to be identified as
the author of this work has been asserted by him
in accordance with the Copyright, Designs and
Patents Act 1988.

This edition published in Great Britain in 2000 by
Millennium
An imprint of Victor Gollancz
Orion House, 5 Upper St Martin's Lane,
London WC2H 9EA

ANDY WARHOL'S DRACULA first published by Victor Gollancz in
2000 as part of FOURSIGHT, edited and with an introduction
by Peter Crowther

To receive information on the Millennium list, e-mail us at:
smy@orionbooks.co.uk

A CIP catalogue record for this book is
available from the British Library

ISBN 1 85798 760 8

Typeset by SetSystems Ltd, Saffron Walden, Essex
Printed in Great Britain by Clays Ltd, St Ives plc

For Sara and Randy
Kim Newman

As Nancy snuffed, her blood curdled. The taste of the vile scabs flooded his mouth. He pushed her away, detaching fangs from her worn wounds. Ropes of bloody spittle hung from her neck to his maw. He wiped his mouth on his wrist, breaking their liquid link. A last electric thrill shuddered, arcing between them. Her heart stopped.

He had pulled her backward onto the bed, holding her down on him as he worked at her throat, her hands feebly scrabbling his sides. Empty, she was deadweight on top of him. He was uncomfortably aware of the other garbage in the bed: magazines, bent spoons, hypodermic needles, used Kleenex, ripped and safety-pinned clothes, banknotes, congealed sandwiches, weeks of uneaten complimentary mints. A package of singles – Sid's 'My Way' – had broken under them, turning the much-stained mattress into a fakir's bed of nails. Vinyl shards stabbed his unbroken skin.

Johnny Pop was naked but for leopard-pattern briefs and socks, and the jewellery. Prizing his new clothes too much to get them gory, he had neatly folded and placed the suit and shirt on a chair well away from the bed. His face and chest were sticky with blood and other discharges.

As the red rush burst in his eyes and ears, his senses flared, more acute by a dozenfold. Outside, in iced velvet October night, police sirens sounded like the wailings of the bereaved mothers of Europe. Distant shots burst as if they were fired in the room, stabs of noise inside his skull. Blobby TV light painted neon a cityscape across ugly wallpaper, populated by psychedelic cockroaches.

He tasted the ghosts of the Chelsea Hotel: drag queens and vampire killers, junkies and pornographers, artists and freaks, visionaries and wasters. Pressing into his mind, they tried to make of his undead body a channel through which they could claw their way back to this plane of existence. Their voices shrieked, clamouring for attention. Cast out of Manhattan, they lusted for restoration to their paved paradise.

Though his throat protested, Johnny forced himself to swallow. Nancy's living blood had scarcely been of better quality than this dead filth. Americans fouled their bodies. Her habits would have killed her soon, even if she hadn't invited a vampire into Room 100. He didn't trouble himself with guilt. Some people were looking for their vampires, begging all their lives for death. His *nosferatu* hold upon the world was tenuous. He could only remain on sufferance. Without the willing warm, he would starve and die. They fed him. They were to blame for him.

Dead blood, heavy with Tuinol and Dilaudid, smote his

brain, washing away the ghosts. He had to be careful; this city was thronged with the truly dead, loitering beyond the ken of the warm, desperate for attention from those who could perceive them. When he was feeding, they crowded around. Having been dead, however briefly, he was a beacon for them.

He yowled and threw the meat-sack off him. He sat up in the bed, nerves drawn taut, and looked at the dead girl. She was ghost-white flesh in black underwear. The flowering neck wound was the least of the marks on her. Scarifications criss-crossed her concave tummy. Pulsing slits opened like gills in her sides, leaking the last of her. The marks of his talons, they were dead mouths, beseeching more kisses from him.

Since arriving in America, he'd been careful to take only those who asked for it, who were already living like ghosts. They had few vampires here. Drained corpses attracted attention. Already, he knew, he'd been noticed. To prosper, he must practise the skills of his father-in-darkness. First, to hide; then, to master.

The Father was always with him, first among the ghosts. He watched over Johnny and kept him from real harm.

Sid, Belsen-thin but for his Biafra-bloat belly, was slumped in a ratty chair in front of blurry early early television. He looked at Johnny and at Nancy, incapable of focusing. Earlier, he'd shot up through his eyeball. Colours slid and flashed across his bare, scarred-and-scabbed chest and arms. His head was a skull in a spiky fright-wig, huge eyes swarming as *Jose and the Pussycats*

3

reflected on the screen of his face. The boy tried to laugh but could only shake. A silly little knife, not even silver, was loosely held in his left hand.

Johnny pressed the heels of his fists to his forehead, and jammed his eyes shut. Bloodred light shone through the skin curtains of his eyelids. He had felt this before. It wouldn't last more than a few seconds. Hell raged in his brain. Then, as if a black fist had struck him in the gullet, peristaltic movement forced fluid up through his throat. He opened his mouth, and a thin squirt of black liquid spattered across the carpet and against the wall.

'Magic spew,' said Sid, in amazement.

The impurities were gone. Johnny was on a pure blood-high now. He contained all of Nancy's short life. She had been an all-American girl. She had given him everything.

He considered the boy in the chair and the girl on the bed, the punks. Their tribes were at war, his and theirs. Clothes were their colours, Italian suits versus safety-pinned PVC pants. This session at the Chelsea had been a truce that turned into a betrayal, a rout, a massacre. The Father was proud of Johnny's strategy.

Sid looked at Nancy's face. Her eyes were open, showing only veined white. He gestured with his knife, realising something had happened. At some point in the evening, Sid had stuck his knife into himself a few times. The tang of his rotten blood filled the room. Johnny's fangs slid from their gum-sheaths, but he had no more hunger yet. He was too full.

He thought of the punks as Americans, but Sid was

English. A musician, though he couldn't really play his guitar. A singer, though he could only shout.

America was a strange new land. Stranger than Johnny had imagined in the Old Country, stranger than he could have imagined. If he drank more blood, he would soon be an American. Then he would be beyond fear, untouchable. It was what the Father wanted for him.

He rolled the corpse off his shins, and cleaned himself like a cat, contorting his supple back and neck, extending his foot-long tongue to lick off the last of the bloodstains. He unglued triangles of vinyl from his body and threw them away. Satisfied, he got off the bed and pulled on crusader white pants, immodestly tight around crotch and rump, loose as a sailor's below the knee. The dark purple shirt settled on his back and chest, sticking to him where his saliva was still wet. He rattled the cluster of gold chains and medallions – Transylvanian charms, badges of honour and conquest – that hung in the gap between his hand-sized collar-points.

With the white jacket, lined in blood-red silk, Johnny was a blinding apparition. He didn't need a strobe to shine in the dark. Sid raised his knife-hand, to cover his eyes. The boy's reaction was better than any mirror.

'Punk sucks,' said Johnny, inviting a response.

'Disco's stupid,' Sid sneered back.

Sid was going to get in trouble. Johnny had to make a slave of the boy, to keep himself out of the story.

He found an unused needle on the bed. Pinching the nipple-like bulb, he stuck the needle into his wrist, spearing the vein perfectly. He let the bulb go and a measure of his blood – of Nancy's? – filled the glass phial. He unstuck himself. The tiny wound was invisibly healed by the time he'd smeared away the bead of blood and licked his thumbprint. He tossed the syrette to Sid, who knew exactly what to do with it, jabbing it into an old arm-track and squirting. Vampire blood slid into Sid's system, something between a virus and a drug. Johnny felt the hook going into Sid's brain, and fed him some line.

Sid stood, momentarily invincible, teeth sharpening, eyes reddened, ears bat-flarred, movements swifter. Johnny shared his sense of power, almost paternally. The vampire buzz wouldn't last long, but Sid would be a slave as long as he lived, which was unlikely to be forever. To become *nosferatu*, you had to give and receive blood; for centuries, most mortals had merely been giving; here, a fresh compact between the warm and the undead was being invented.

Johnny nodded towards the empty thing on the bed. Nobody's blood was any good to her now. He willed the command through the line, through the hook, into Sid's brain. The boy, briefly possessed, leaped across the room, landing on his knees on the bed, and stuck his knife into the already dead girl, messing up the wounds on her throat, tearing open her skin in dozens of places. As he slashed, Sid snarled, black fangs splitting his gums.

Johnny let himself out of the room.

*

They were calling him a vampire long before he turned.

*At the Silver Dream Factory, the Mole People, amphetamine-swift dusk-til-dawners eternally out for blood, nicknamed him 'Drella': half-Dracula, half-Cinderella. The coven often talked of Andy's 'victims': first, cast-offs whose lives were appropriated for Art, rarely given money to go with their limited fame (a great number of them now truly dead); later, wealthy portrait subjects or **Inter/VIEW** advertisers, courted as assiduously as any Renaissance art patron (a great number of them ought to be truly dead). Andy leached off them all, left them drained or transformed, using them without letting them touch him, never distinguishing between the commodities he could only coax from other people: money, love, blood, inspiration, devotion, death. Those who rated him a genius and those who ranked him a fraud reached eagerly, too eagerly, for the metaphor. It was so persistent, it must eventually become truth.*

*In Swimming Underground: My Years in the Warhol Factory (1995), supervamp Mary Woronov (**Hedy/The Shoplifter**, 1965; **The Chelsea Girls**, 1966) writes: 'People were calling us the undead, vampires, me and my little brothers of the night, with our lips pressed against the neck of the city, sucking the energy out of scene after scene. We left each party behind like a wasted corpse, raped and carelessly tossed aside ... Andy was the worst, taking on five and six parties a night. He even looked like a vampire: white, empty, waiting to be filled, incapable of satisfaction. He was the white worm — always hungry, always cold, never still, always twisting.' When told that the artist had actually turned vampire, Lou Reed arched a ragged eyebrow and quizzed, 'Andy was **alive**?' In* *the multitude of memoirs and word or song portraits that try to define Andy Warhol, there is no instance of anyone ever using the adjective 'warm' about him.*

Valerie Solanas, who prompted Andy's actual turning, took superstitious care to shoot him with homemade silver bullets. She tried wrapping .32 ammunition in foil, which clogged the chambers, before resorting to spray-paint in the style of Billy Name (Linich), the silver-happy decorator of the Factory who coffined himself in a tiny back-room for two years, coming out only at dead of night to forage. The names are just consonants short of anagrams: Andy Warhola, Wlad Draculya; Valerie Solanas, Van Helsing. Valerie's statement, the slogan of a fearless vampire killer: 'he had too much control over my life.' On the operating table – 4.51 pm, Monday, June 3, 1968 – Andy Warhol's heart stopped. He was declared clinically dead but came back and lived on, his vision of death and disaster fulfilled and survived. The stringmeat ghost of the latter years was sometimes a parody of his living self, a walking Diane Arbus exhibit, belly scars like zippers, Ray-Ban eyes and dead skin.

*Warhola the Vampyre sloped **nosferatu**-taloned through the seventies, a fashion-setter as always, as – after nearly a century in the open in Europe – vampirism (of a sort) at last established itself in America. He had no get, but was the fountainhead of a bloodline. You can still see them, in galleries or **People**, on the streets after dark, in the clubs and cellars. Andy's kids: cloned creatures, like the endless replications of his silkscreen celebrity portraits, faces repeated until they become meaningless patterns of colour dots. When alive, Andy had said he wanted to become* *a machine and that everybody should be alike. How did he feel when his wishes were coming true? How did he feel about anything? Did he feel? Ever? If you spend any amount of time trying to understand the man and his work, you can't help but worry that he's reaching from beyond the grave and forcing you to become Valerie.*

Consider the signs, the symptoms, the symbols: that pale, almost-albino face, simultaneously babyish and ancient, shrinking like a bucket of salted slugs when exposed to the sun; the sharp or battered black clothes, stiff from the grave; the goggle-like dark glasses, hypnotic black holes where eyes should be; the slavic monotone of the whispery voice and the pared-down, kindergarten vocabulary; the covert religiosity, the prizing of sacred or silver objects; the squirrelling-away of money and possessions in a centuried lair; even the artificial shocks of grey-white-silver hair. Are these not the attributes of a classical vampire, Dracula himself? Look at photographs taken before or after June 1968, and you can't tell whether he is or isn't. Like the murgatroyds of the 1890s, Andy was a disciple before he became a vampire. For him, turning was dropping the seventh veil, the last chitinous scrap of chrysalis, a final stage in becoming what he had always meant to be, an admittal that this was indeed what was inside him.

His whole life had revolved around the dead.

Kathleen Conklin,
'Destroying Drella', *paper delivered at 'Warhol's Worlds', inaugural conference of The Andy Warhol Museum (April 21–23, 1995); revised for publication as 'Warhola the Vampyre' in* **Who is Andy Warhol?**, *edited by Colin MacCabe*

with Mark Francis and Peter Wollen (The British Film Institute and The Andy Warhol Museum, 1997).

He stepped out of the Chelsea Hotel onto the sidewalk of West 23rd Street, and tasted New York. It was the dead time, the thick hours before dawn, when all but the most committed night owls were home abed, or at least crashed out on a floor, blood sluggish with coffee, cigarettes or drugs. This was the vampire afternoon, and Johnny understood how alone he was. There were other vampires in this city, and he was almost ready to seek them out, but none like him, of his line.

America was vast, bloated with rich, fatty blood. The fresh country supported only a few ticks that tentatively poked probosces through thick hide, sampling without gorging. By comparison, Johnny was a hungry monster. Minutes after taking Nancy, he could have fed again, and again. He had to take more than he needed. He could handle dozens of warm bodies a night without bursting, without choking on the ghosts. Eventually, he would make children-in-darkness, slaves to serve him, to shield him. He must pass on the bloodline of the Father. But not yet.

He hadn't intended to come to this city of towers, with its moat of running water. His plan was to stick to the film people he had hooked up with in the Old Country, and go to fabled Hollywood on the Pacific. But there was a mix-up at JFK and he was detained in Immigration while the rest of the company, American passports brandished like protective banners, were waved on to catch connecting flights to Los Angeles or San Francisco. He was stuck at the airport in a crowd of overeager petitioners, dark-skinned and warm, as dawn edged threateningly closer. The Father was with him then, as he slipped into a Men's Room and bled a Canadian flight attendant who gave him a come-on, invigorating himself with something new and wild. Buzzing with fresh blood, first catch of this new land, he concentrated his powers of fascination to face down the officials who barred his way. It was beneath him to bribe those who could be overpowered by force of will.

America was disorienting. To survive, he must adapt swiftly. The pace of change in this century was far more rapid than the glacial shifts of the long years the Father had in his Carpathian fastness. Johnny would have to surpass the Father to keep ahead, but bloodline would tell. Though of an ancient line, he was a 20th Century creature, turned only thirty-five years earlier, taken into the dark before he was formed as a living man. In Europe, he had been a boy, hiding in the shadows, waiting. Here, in this bright America, he could fulfil his potential. People took him for a young man, not a child.

Johnny Pop had arrived.

He knew he had been noticed. He was working hard to fit in, but recognised how gauche he had been a few short weeks ago. On his first nights in New York, he had made mistakes. Blood in the water excited the sharks.

Someone stood on the corner, watching him. Two black men, in long leather coats. One wore dark glasses despite the hour, the other had a slim-brimmed hat with a tiny feather in the band. Not vampires, there was something of the predator about them. They were well-armed. Silver shoe-buckles and buttons, coats loose over guns. And their bodies were weapons, a finished blade, an arrow shaft. From inside his coat, the black man in sunglasses produced a dark knife. Not silver, but polished hardwood.

Johnny tensed, ready to fight and kill. He had just fed. He was at his strongest.

The knifeman smiled. He balanced his weapon by its point, and tapped his forehead with its hilt, a warrior salute. He would not attack yet. His presence was an announcement, a warning. He was showing himself. This man had seen Johnny before he was seen. His night-skills were sharp.

Then, the knifeman and his partner were gone. They had seemed to disappear, to step into a shadow even Johnny's night eyes could not penetrate.

He suppressed a shudder. This city was not yet his jungle, and he was exposed here – out on the street in a white suit that shone like a beacon – as he had not been in the Old Country.

The black men should have destroyed him now. When they had a chance. Johnny would do his best to see they did not get another.

It was time to move on, to join the crowd.

A mustard-yellow taxi cruised along the street, emerging like a dragon from an orange-pink groundswell of steam. Johnny hailed the cab, and slid into its cage-like interior. The seat was criss-crossed with duct tape, battlefield dressings on a fatal wound. The driver, a gaunt white man with a baggy military jacket, looked instinctively at the rear-view mirror, expecting to lock eyes with his fare. Johnny saw surprise in the young man's face as he took in the reflection of an empty hack. He twisted to look into the dark behind him and saw Johnny there, understanding at once what he had picked up.

'You have a problem?' Johnny asked.

After a moment, the taxi driver shrugged.

'Hell, no. A lot of guys won't even take spooks, but I'll take anyone. They all come out at night.'

Behind the driver's gunsight eyes, Johnny saw jungle twilight, purpled by napalm blossoms. He heard the reports of shots fired years ago. His nostrils stung with dead cordite.

Uncomfortable, he broke the connection.

Johnny told the driver to take him to Studio 54.

Even now, this late in the night, a desperate line lingered outside the club. Their breaths frosted in a cloud, and they stamped unfashionably-shoed feet against the cold. Losers with no chance, they would cajole and plead with Burns and Stu, the hard-faced bouncers, but never see the velvet rope lifted. An invisible sign was on their foreheads. Worse than dead, they were boring.

Johnny paid off the cab with sticky bills lifted from Nancy's purse, and stood on the sidewalk, listening to the throb of the music from inside. 'Pretty Baby', Blondie. Debbie Harry's living dead voice called to him.

The taxi did not move off. Was the driver hoping for

another fare from among these damned? No, he was fixing Johnny in his mind. A man without a reflection should be remembered.

'See you again soon, Jack,' said the white man.

Like the black men outside the Chelsea, the taxi driver was a danger. Johnny had marked him. It was good to know who would come for you, to be prepared. The white man's name was written on his licence just as his purpose was stamped on his face. It was Travis. In Vietnam, he had learned to look monsters in the face, even in the mirror.

The cab snarled to life and prowled off.

Moving with the music, Johnny crossed the sidewalk towards the infernal doorway, reaching out with his mind to reconnect with the bouncers, muscular guys with Tom of Finland leather caps and jackets. Burns was a moonlighting cop with sad eyes and bruises, Stu a trust fund kid with his own monster father in his head; Johnny's hooks were in both of them, played out on the thinnest of threads. They were not, would never be, his get, but they were his. First, he would have warm chattels; get would come later.

He enjoyed the wails and complaints from losers as he breezed past the line, radiating an 'open sesame' they could never manage. Stu clicked the studded heels of his motorcycle boots and saluted, fingers aligned with the peak of his black leather forage cap with Austro-Hungarian precision. Burns smartly lifted the rope, the little sound of the hook being detached from the eye exciting envious sighs, and stood aside. To savour the moment,

Johnny paused in the doorway, knowing the spill of light from inside made his suit shine like an angelic raiment, and surveyed those who would never get in. Their eyes showed such desperation that he almost pitied them.

Two weeks ago, he had been among them, drawn to the light but kept away from the flame. Like some older creatures of his kind, he could not force his way into a place until he had been invited across the threshold. Then, his clothes – found in a suitcase chosen at random from the carousel at the airport – had not been good. Being *nosferatu* was unusual enough to get him attention. Steve Rubell was passing the door, and took note of Johnny's sharp, beautiful face. Possessed of the knack of seeing himself as others saw him, Johnny understood the owner-manager was intrigued by the vampire boy on his doorstep. But Shining Lucifer himself couldn't get into 54 with a Bicentennial shirt, cowboy boots and black hair flattened like wet sealskin to his skull.

When he came back, the next night, he wore clothes that fit: a Halston suit – black outside in the dark, with a violet weave that showed under the lights – and a Ralph Lauren shirt with fresh bloodstains across the polo player. They still smelled faintly of their previous owner, Tony from Brooklyn. The bouncers didn't even need to check with Steve to let Johnny in, and he took the opportunity, later that night in the back rooms, to lay a tiny smear of his blood on them both, apparently a token of gratitude, actually a sigil of ownership. Johnny was saving them for later, knowing they would be needed.

As he ducked past the curtains and slid into 54, Johnny

felt Tony's ghost in his limbs. He had taken much from Tony Manero, whom he had exsanguinated on the Brooklyn Bridge. From the boy, he had caught the blood rhythms that matched the music of the month. Tony had been a dancer; Johnny had inherited that from him, along with his fluffed-up but flared-back hairstyle and clothes that were not just a protective cover but a style, a display.

Tony was with him most nights now, a ghost. The kid had never made it to 54, but he'd been better than Brooklyn, good enough for Manhattan. Johnny thought Tony, whose empty carcass he had weighted and tossed off the Bridge, would be happy that some of him at least had made it in the real city. When the blood was still fresh in him, Johnny had followed its track, back to Tony's apartment, and slipped in – unnoticed by the kid's family, even the fallen priest – to take away his wardrobe, the night-clothes that were now his armour.

He let the music take him, responding to it with all his blood. Nancy's ghost protested, making puking motions at the sound of the disco despised by all true punks. By taking her, Johnny had won a great victory in the style wars. He liked killing punks. No one noticed when they were gone. They were all committing slow suicide anyway; that was the point, for there was no future. To love disco was to want to live forever, to aspire to an immortality of consumption. Punks didn't believe in anything beyond death, and loved nothing, not even themselves.

He wondered what would happen to Sid.

A man in the moon puppet, spooning coke up his

nose, beamed down from the wall, blessing the throng with a 1978 benediction. As Johnny stepped onto the illuminated floor and strutted through the dancers, his suit shone like white flame. He had the beat with his every movement. Even his heart pulsed in time to the music. He smiled as he recognised the song, fangs bright as neons under the strobe, eyes red glitterballs. This was the music he had made his own, the song that meant the most of all the songs.

'Staying Alive', The Bee Gees.

In its chorus, he heard the wail of the warm as they died under his kisses, ah-ah-ah-ah, staying alive. In its lyric, he recognised himself, a woman's man with no time to talk.

His dancing cleared a circle.

It was like feeding. Without even taking blood, he drew in the blood of the crowd to himself, loosening the ghosts of those who danced with him from their bodies. Tulpa spirits stretched out through mouths and noses and attached to him like ectoplasmic straws. As he danced, he sucked with his whole body, tasting minds and hearts, outshining them all. No one came near, to challenge him. The Father was proud of him.

For the length of the song, he *was* alive.

*Andrew Warhola was an American — born in Pittsburgh on August 6th, 1928 — but his family were not. In **The Life and Death of Andy Warhol** (1989), Victor Bockris quotes his statement 'I am from nowhere', but gives it the lie: 'The Warholas were Rusyns who had emigrated to America from the*

17

Ruthenian village of Mikova in the Carpathian Mountains near the borders of Russia and Poland in territory that was, at the turn of the century, part of the Austro-Hungarian Empire'. Bockris takes care, introducing early the theme that comes to dominate his biography, to note 'The Carpathian Mountains are popularly known as the home of Dracula, and the peasants in Jonathan Harker's description kneeling before roadside shrines, crossing themselves at the mention of Dracula's name, resemble Andy Warhol's distant relatives.'

The third son of Ondrej and Julia Warhola grew up in Soho, an ethnic enclave that was almost a ghetto. From an early age, he seemed a changeling, paler and slighter than his family, laughably unfit for a future in the steel mills, displaying talent as soon as his hand could properly hold a pencil. Others in his situation might fantasise that they were orphaned princes, raised by peasant wood-cutters, but the Warholas had emigrated – escaped? – from the land of the vampires. Not fifty years before, Count Dracula had come out of Carpathia and established his short-lived empire in London. Dracula was still a powerful figure then, the most famous vampire in the world, and his name was spoken often in the Warhola household. Years later, in a film, Andy had an actress playing his mother claim to have been a victim, in childhood, of the Count, that Dracula's bloodline remained in her veins, passing in the womb to her last son. Like much else in Andy's evolving autobiography, there is no literal truth in this story but its hero spent years trying to wish it into reality and may even, at the last, have managed to pull off the trick. Before settling on 'Andy Warhol' as his eventual professional name, he experimented with the signature 'Andrew Alucard'.

Julia was horrified by her little Andrew's inclinations. For her, vampires were objects not of fascination but dread. A devout Byzantine Catholic, she would drag her children six miles to the wooden church of St John Chrystostom's on Saline Street and subject them to endless rituals of purification. Yet, among Andy's first drawings are bats and coffins. In the 1930s, as Dracula held court in one of his many exiles, the American illustrated press were as obsessed with vampires as movie stars. There were several successful periodicals – **Weird Tales, Spicy Vampire Stories** *– devoted almost entirely to their social activities. To look through these magazines, as the child Andy did, is to understand what it is to learn that a party is going on after your bedtime, to which you cannot possibly secure an invitation. Literally, you had to die to get in. In Vienna, Budapest, Constantinople, Monte Carlo and private estates and castles scattered in a crescent across Europe, vampire kings and queens held court.*

Young Andrew clipped photographs and portraits from the magazines and hoarded them for the rest of his life. He preferred photographs, especially the blurred or distorted traces of those who barely registered on cameras or in mirrors. He understood at once that creatures denied the sight of their own faces must prize portrait painters. He wrote what might be called 'fan letters' to the leaders of vampire fashion: de Lioncourt of Paris, Andrew Bennett of London, the White Russian Rozokov. His especial favourites among the undead, understandably, were the child-vampires, those frozen infant immortals Noel Coward sings about in 'Poor Little Dead Girl'. His prize possession as a boy was an autographed portrait of the martyred Claudia, ward of the stylish de Lioncourt, considered

...gon and an archetype among her kind. He would later ...se this image – a subscription gift sent out by **Night Life** – in his silkscreen, **Vampire Doll** (1963).

In his fascination with the undead, Andy was in the avant-garde. There were still very few vampires in America, and those American-born or -made tended to flee to a more congenial Europe. There was a vampire panic in the wake of the First World War, as returning veterans brought back the tainted bloodline that burned out in the epidemic of 1919. The lost generation new-borns, who all incubated within their bodies a burning disease that ate them up from the inside within months, were ghastly proof that vampires would never 'take' in the New World. Congress passed acts against the spread of vampirism save under impossibly regulated circumstances. J. Edgar Hoover ranked vampires just below communists and well above organised crime as a threat to the American way of life. In the 1930s, New York District Attorney Thomas Dewey led a crusade against an influx of Italian vampires, successfully deporting coven-leader Niccolo Cavalanti and his acolytes. In the South, a resurgence of the Ku Klux Klan viciously curbed a potential renaissance of interlocked vampire **hounforts** in New Orleans and throughout the bayou country.

America, like Julia Warhola, considered all vampires loathsome monsters. Yet, as Andy understood, there was a dreadful glamour. During the Depression, glimpses of the high life lived in another continent and by another species, seemed enticing. The Hungarian Paul Lukas was the first Hollywood actor to specialise in undead roles, from **Scarface** (1932) to **The House of Ruthven** (1937). A few real vampires, even, made it in the movies: Garbo, Malakai, Chevalier Futaine. With the rise of *fascism and the Second World War came a trickle of vampire refugees from the Old World. Laws were revised and certain practices tolerated 'for the duration', while Hoover's FBI — constantly nagged by America's witch-hunters Cardinal Spellman and Father Coughlin — compiled foot-thick dossiers on elders and new-borns alike. As Nazi eugenicists strived to cleanse his bloodline from the Reich, Dracula himself aligned with the Allies, and a vampire underground in occupied Europe co-operated with the liberating forces.*

*When the War was over, the climate changed again and a round of blacklistings, arrests and show-trials — notably the prosecution for treason of American-born and -made vampire Benjamin Lathem by Robert F. Kennedy — drove all but those who could 'pass for warm' back to Europe. That was the era of the scare movies, with homburg-hatted government men taking crucifix and stake to swarthy, foreign infiltrators: **I Married a Vampire** (1950), **I was a Vampire for the FBI** (1951), **Blood of Dracula** (1958). Warhol was in New York by now, sketching shoes for ad lay-outs or arranging window displays for Bonwit Teller's, making a hundred thousand dollars a year but fretting that he wasn't taken seriously. Money wasn't enough for him; he needed to be famous too, as if under the curse described by Fritz Leiber in 'The Casket Demon' (1963) — unless known of and talked about, he would fade to nothingness. Like America, he had not outgrown his vampire craze, just learned to keep quiet about it.*

*In 1956, the year **Around the World in 80 Days** took the Best Picture Oscar, Andy took an extended trip with the frustratingly unforthcoming Charles Lisanby — Hawaii, Japan, India, Egypt, Rome, Paris, London. Throughout that itinerary,* *he saw vampires living openly, mingling with the warm, as adored as they were feared. Is it too much to suppose that, in a maharajah's palace or on a Nile paddle-wheeler, spurned by Charles and driven to abase himself before some exotic personage, he was bitten?*

Conklin, *ibid*

'Gee, who is that boy?' asked Andy, evenly. 'He is fantastic.'

Penelope was used to the expression. It was one of Andy's few adjectives. Everyone and everything was either 'fantastic' or 'a bore' or something similar, always with an elongated vowel early on. All television was 'fa-antastic'; World War II was 'a bo-ore'. Vintage cookie tins were 'si-imply wonderful'; income taxes were 'ra-ather old'. Famous people were 've-ery interesting'; living daylight was 'pra-ctically forgotten'.

She turned to look down on the dance floor. They were sitting up on the balcony, above the churning masses, glasses of chilled blood on the table between them, at once shadowed enough to be mysterious and visible enough to be recognisable. There was no point in coming to Studio 54 unless it was to be seen, to be noticed. At tomorrow's sunset, when they both rose from their day's sleep, it would be Penny's duty to go through the columns, reading out any mentions of their appearances, so Andy could cluck and crow over what was said about him, and lament that so much was left out.

It took her a moment to spot the object of Andy's attention.

For once, he was right. The dancer in the white suit was fantastic. Fa-antastic, even. She knew at once that the boy was like her, *nosferatu*. His look, his style, was American, but she scented a whiff of European grave-mould. This was no new-born, no *nouveau*, but an experienced creature, practised in his dark-skills. Only a vampire with many nights behind him could seem so *young*.

It had to happen. She was not the first to come here. She had known an invasion was inevitable. American could not hold out forever. She had not come here to be unique, but to be away from her kind, from her former lives. Though she had inevitably hooked up with Andy, she did not want to be sucked back into the world of the undead. But what she wanted meant very little any more, which was as it should be. Whatever came, she would accept. It was her duty, her burden.

She looked back at Andy. It took sharp senses indeed to distinguish his real enthusiasms from his feigned ones. He had worked hard – and it did not do to underestimate this languid scarecrow's capacity for hard work – to become as inexpressive as he was, to cultivate what passed in America for a lack of accent. His chalk-dusted cheeks and cold mouth gave nothing away. His wig was silver tonight, thick and stiff as a knot of fox-tails. His suit was quiet, dark and Italian, worn with a plain tie.

They both wore goggle-like black glasses to shield their eyes from the club's frequent strobes. But, unlike some of his earlier familiars, Penny made no real attempt to look like him.

She watched the dancer spin, hip-cocked, arm raised in a disco heil, white jacket flaring to show scarlet lining, a snarl of concentration on his cold lovely face.

How could Andy not be interested in another of the undead? Especially one like this.

At least the dancing boy meant the night wasn't a complete wash-out. It had been pretty standard, so far: two openings, three parties and a reception. One big disappointment: Andy had hoped to bring Miz Lillian, the President's mama, to the reception for Princess Ashraf, twin sister of the Shah of Iran, but the White House got wind and scuttled the plan. Andy's fall-back date, Lucie Arnaz, was hardly a substitute, and Penny was forced to make long conversation with the poor girl – whom she had never heard of – while Andy did the silent act most people thought of as deliberate mystification but which was actually simply sulking. The Princess, sharp ornament of one of the few surviving vampire ruling houses, was not exactly on her finest fettle, either – preoccupied by the troubles of her absolutist brother, who was currently back home surrounded by Mohammedan fanatics screaming for his impalement.

In the car between Bianca Jagger's party at the Tea Rooms and L. B. Jeffries's opening at the Photographers' Gallery, Paloma Picasso rather boringly went on about the tonic properties of human blood as face cream. Penny would have told the warm twit how stupid she was being about matters of which she plainly knew nothing, but Andy was frozen enough already without his faithful vampire conpanion teeing off someone so famous –

Penny wasn't sure what exactly the painter's daughter was famous *for* – she was sure to get his name in *Vanity Fair*. At Bianca's, Andy thought he'd spotted Davie Bowie with Catherine Deneuve, but it turned out to be a far less interesting couple. Another disappointment.

Bob Colacello, editor of *Inter/VIEW* and Andy's connection with the Pahlavis, wittered on about how well the Princess was bearing up, and was trying to sell him on committing to an exhibition in the new museum of modern art the Shah had endowed in Teheran. Penny could tell Andy was chilling on the idea, sensing – quite rightly – that it would not do well to throw in with someone on the point of losing everything. Andy elaborately ignored Bob, and that meant everyone else did too. He had been delighted to learn from her what 'being sent to Coventry' meant and redoubled his use of that ancient schoolboy torture. There was a hurt desperation in Bob's chatter, but it was all his own fault and she didn't feel a bit sorry for him.

At the Photographers', surrounded by huge blow-ups of war orphans and devastated Asian villages, Andy got on one of his curiosity jags and started quizzing her, Penny, about Oscar Wilde. What had he been like, had he really been amusing all the time, had he been frightened when the wolves gathered, how much had he earned, how famous had he really been, would he have been recognised everywhere he went? After nearly a hundred years, she remembered Wilde less than many others she had known in the '80s. Like her, the poet was one of the first modern generation of new-born vampires. He was one of those who turned but didn't last more than a decade, eaten up by disease carried over from warm life. She didn't like to think of contemporaries she had outlived. But Andy insisted, nagging, and she dutifully coughed up anecdotes and aphorisms to keep him contented. She told Andy that he reminded her of Oscar, which was certainly true in some ways. Penny dreaded being recategorised from 'fascinating' to 'a bore', with the consequent casting into the outer darkness.

All her life, all her afterlife, had been spent by her own choice in the shadows cast by a succession of tyrants. She supposed she was punishing herself for her sins. Andy had noticed; in the Factory, she was called 'Penny Penance' or 'Penny Penitent'. However, besotted with titles and honours, he usually introduced her to outsiders as 'Penelope Churchward, Lady Godalming'. She had never been married to Lord Godalming (or, indeed, anyone), but Arthur Holmwood had been her father-in-darkness, and some vampire aristos did indeed pass on titles to their get.

She was not the first English rose in Andy's entourage. She had been told she looked like the model Jane Forth, who had been in Andy's movies. Penny knew she had only become Andy's Girl of the Year after Catherine Guinness left the Factory to become Lady Neidpath. She had an advantage over Andy's earlier debs, though: she was never going to get old. As Girl of the Year, it was her duty to be Andy's companion of the night and to handle much of the organisational and social business of the Factory, of Andy Warhol Enterprises, Incorporated. It was something she was used to, from her Victorian years as an 'Angel in the Home' to her nights as last governess of the House of Dracula. She could even keep track of the money.

She sipped her blood, decanted from some bar worker who was 'really' an actor or a model. Andy left his drink untouched, as usual. He didn't trust blood that showed up in a glass, and nobody ever saw him feeding. Penny wondered if he were an abstainer. Just now, the red pinpoints in his dark glasses were fixed. He was still watching the dancer.

The vampire in the white suit hooked her attention too.

For a moment, she was sure it was *him*, come back yet again, young and lethal, intent on murderous revenge.

She breathed the name, 'Dracula'.

Andy's sharp ears picked it up, even through the dreadful guff that passed for music these days. It was one of the few names guaranteed to provoke his interest.

Andy prized her for her connection to the late King Vampire. Penny had been at the Palazzo Otranto at the end. She was one of the few who knew the truth about the last hours of *il principe*, though she jealously kept that anecdote to herself. It was bad enough that the memories lingered.

'The boy looks like him,' she said. 'He might be the Count's get, or of his bloodline. Most vampires Dracula made came to look like him. He spread his doppelgängers throughout the world.'

Andy nodded, liking the idea.

The dancer had Dracula's red eyes, his aquiline nose, his full mouth. But he was clean-shaven and had a bouffant of teased black hair, like a Broadway actor or a teenage idol. His look was as much Roman as Romanian.

Penny had understood on their first meeting that Andy Warhol didn't want to be just a vampire. He wanted to be *the* vampire, Dracula. Even before his death and resurrection, his coven had called him 'Drella'. It was meant to be cruel: he was the Count of the night hours, but at dawn he changed back into the girl who cleared away the ashes.

'Find out who he is, Penny,' Andy said. 'We should meet him. He's going to be famous.'

She had no doubt of that.

Flushed from dancing and still buzzed with Nancy's blood, Johnny moved on to the commerce of the night. The first few times, he had set up his shop in men's rooms, like the dealers he was rapidly putting out of business. Spooked by all the mirrors, he shifted from striplit johns to the curtained back rooms where the other action was. All the clubs had such places.

In the dark room, he felt the heat of the busy bodies and tasted ghosts, expelled on yo-yo strings of ectoplasm during orgasm. He threaded his way through writhing limbs to take up his habitual spot in a leather armchair. He slipped off his jacket, draping it carefully over the back of the chair, and popped his cuff-links, rolling his sleeves up to his elbows. His white lower arms and hands shone in the dark.

Burns, on a break, came to him first. The hook throbbed in his brain, jones throbbing in his bones like a slow drumbeat. The first shot of drac had been free, but now it was a hundred dollars a pop. The bouncer handed Johnny a crisp C-note. With the nail of his little finger, Johnny jabbed a centimetre-long cut in the skin of his left arm. Burns knelt down in front of the chair and licked away the welling blood. He began to suckle the wound, and Johnny pushed him away.

There was a plea in the man's eyes. The drac jolt was in him, but it wasn't enough. He had the strength and the senses, but also the hunger.

'Go bite someone,' Johnny said, laughing.

The bouncer's hook was in deep. He loved Johnny and hated him, but he'd do what he said. For Burns, hell would be to be expelled, to be denied forever the taste.

A girl, in a shimmering fringed dress, replaced the bouncer. She had violent orange hair.

'Is it true?' she asked.

'Is what true?'

'That you can make people like you?'

He smiled, sharply. He could make people *love* him.

'A hundred dollars and you can find out,' he said.

'I'm game.'

She was very young, a child. She had to scrape together the notes, in singles and twenties. Usually, he had no patience for that, and pushed such small-timers out of the way to find someone with the right money, as curt as a bus driver. But he needed small bills too, for cabfare and tips.

As her mouth fixed on his fresh wound, he felt his barb sink into her. She was a virgin, in everything. Within seconds, she was his slave. Her eyes widened as she found she was able to see in the dark. She touched fingertips to her suddenly sharp teeth.

It would last such a pathetically short time, but for now she was a princess of the shadows. He named her Nocturna, and made her his daughter until dawn. She floated out of the room, to hunt.

He drew more cuts across his arm, accepted more money, gave more drac. A procession of strangers, all his slaves, passed through. Every night there were more.

After an hour, he had $8,500 in bills. Nancy's ghost was gone, stripped away from him in dribs and drabs, distributed among his children of the night. His veins were sunken and tingling. His mind was crowded with impressions that faded to nothing as fast as the scars on his milky skin. All around, in the dark, his temporary get bit each other. He relished the musical yelps of pain and pleasure.

Now, he thirsted again.

Vampires show up in the 1950s fashion drawings, if only through coded symbols: ragged-edged batwing cloaks, draped over angular figures; red lipstick mouths on sharp-cheeked, black and white faces; tiny, almost unnoticeable, fangs peeping from stretched smiles. These in-jokes are self-criticism, a nervous admission of what had to happen next. To become 'Andy Warhol', the illustrator and window-dresser must die and be reborn as an Artist. Those who accuse him of being concerned only with his earnings – which, to be fair, is what he told anyone who would listen – forget that he abandoned a considerable income to devote all his energies to work which initially lost a lot of money.

Shortly before the Coca-Cola Bottle and Campbell's Soup Can series made him famous, and in a period when he feared he had recovered from one 'nervous breakdown' only to be slipping into another, Warhol did a painting – synthetic polymer and crayon on canvas – of **Batman** (1960), the only vampire ever really to be embraced by America. Though justifiably eclipsed by Lichtenstein's appropriations from comic strip panels, **Batman** is an important work in its own right, an idea seized but abandoned half-finished, the first flash of what would soon come to be called Pop Art. Like much from the period before Warhol hit upon repetition and manufacture as modes of expression, it seems incomplete, childish crayon scribbles across the cowled Bob Kane outline of the classic vampire vigilante. Exhibited at the Castelli Gallery, the work was the first Warhol piece to command a serious price from a private collector – an anonymous buyer on behalf of the Wayne Foundation – which may have encouraged the artist to continue with his personal work.

During an explosion of creativity that began in 1962 and lasted at least until he was shot, Warhol took a lease on a former hat works at 231 East 47th Street and turned the loft space into the Factory, with the intention of producing Art on a production line. At the suggestion of assistant Nathan Gluck, Warhol seized upon the silkscreen process and ('like a forger'), turned out series of dollar bills, soup cans and Marilyn Monroes. It seems that he didn't care what his subjects were, so long *as they were famous. When Henry Geldzahler, Assistant Curator for 20th Century American Art at the Metropolitan Museum, told him he should apply himself to more 'serious' subjects, Warhol began his 'death and disaster' series, images of car crashes, suicides and the electric chair. Straddling the trivial and the serious are his vampire portraits: **Carmilla Karnstein** (1962), **Vampire Doll** (1963), **Lucy Westenra** (1963). Red-eyed and jagged-mouthed undead faces, reproduced in sheets like unperforated stamps, vivid greens and oranges for skin-tones, the series reinvents the 19th Century genre of vampire portraiture. The vampire subjects Andy chose shared one thing: all had been famously destroyed. He produced parallel silkscreens of their true deaths: impalements, decapitations, disintegrations. These are perhaps the first great works, ruined corpses swimming in scarlet blood, untenanted bodies torn apart by grim puritans.*

In 1964, Andy delivered a twenty by twenty black and white mural called 'Thirteen Vampires' to the American pavilion at the New York World's Fair, where it was to be exhibited beside work by Robert Rauschenberg and Roy Lichtenstein. Among the thirteen, naturally, was Warhol's first Dracula portrait, though all the other undead notables represented were women. The architect Philip Johnson, who had commissioned the piece, informed Warhol that word had come from the Governor that it was to be removed because there was concern that it was offensive to the God-fearing. When Warhol's suggestion that the portraits all be defaced with burning crosses to symbolise the triumph of the godly was vetoed, he went out to the fair with Geldzahler and another of his assistants, Gerard Malanga, and painted the mural over with a thick layer of undead-banishing silver paint, declaring 'and that'll be my art'. We can only speculate about the lost Dracula portrait, which none of the few who saw it can describe in detail. Which of the many, many images of the King of the Vampires – then truly dead for only five years – did Warhol reproduce? The most tantalising suggestion, based on Malanga's later-retracted version, is that for the only time in his entire career as an Artist, Warhol drew on his own imagination rather than copied or reproduced from life. Andy lied constantly, but this is the only occasion when anyone has ever accused him of **making something up**.

Warhol's first experiments with film, conducted in real-time with the co-opted collaboration of whoever happened to be hanging about in the Factory, are steeped in the atmosphere of vampirism. The camera hovers over the exposed throat of John Giorno in **Sleep** (1963) as if ready to pounce. The projection of film shot at twenty-four frames per second at the silent speed of sixteen frames per second gives Giorno's six-hour night a suggestion of vampire lassitude. The flashes of white leader that mark the change of shots turn dirty sheets into white coffin plush, and the death rattle of the projector is the only sound-track (aside from the comical yawns and angry ticket-money-back demands of any audience members happening upon the film in a real theatre). That same year, Warhol shot more explicit studies of vampirism: in **Kiss**, a succession of couples osculate like insects unable to uncouple their complex mouth-parts; in **Eat**, Robert Indiana crams his mouth with unidenti-fiable meats; and **Suck-Job** is an extended (thirty minutes) close-up of the face of a young man who is being nibbled by beings who never intrude into the frame or register on film. For **Suck-Job**, Warhol had arranged with Alex Ford, a real

*vampire, to 'appear' but Ford didn't take him seriously and
failed to show up at the Factory for the shoot, forcing the artist
to substitute pasty-faced but warm hustlers dragged off the
street.*

*When Warhol turned his camera on the Empire State Build-
ing in* **Empire** *(1964), it saw the edifice first as the largest
coffin in the world, jutting out of the ground as if dislodged by
some seismic activity. As night slowly falls and the floodlights
come on, the building becomes a cloaked predator standing
colossal over New York City, shoulders sloped by the years, head
sprouting a dirigible-mast horn. After that, Warhol had fellow
underground filmmaker Jack Smith swish a cape over Baby
Jane Hudson in the now-lost* **Batman Dracula** *(1964). Only
tantalising stills, of Smith with a mouthful of plastic teeth and
staring Lon Chaney eyes, remain of his film, which – as with
the silver-coated 'Thirteen Vampires' – is perhaps as Andy
wanted it. As with* **Sleep** *and* **Empire**, *the idea is more
important than the artefact. It is enough that the films exist;
they are not meant actually to be seen all the way through.
When Jonas Mekas scheduled* **Empire** *at the Filmmakers' Co-
Op in 1965, he lured Warhol into the screening room and tied
him securely to one of the seats with stout rope, intent on forcing
the creator to sit through his creation. When he came back two
hours later to check up, he found Warhol had chewed through
his bonds – briefly, an incarnation of* **Batman Dracula** *– and
escaped into the night. In the early sixties, Warhol had begun
to file his teeth, sharpening them to piranha-like needle-points.*

    Conklin, *ibid*

*

A red-headed vampire girl bumped into her and hissed, displaying pearly fangs. Penelope lowered her dark glasses and gave the chit a neon glare. Cowed, the creature backed away. Intrigued, Penny took the girl by the bare upper arm, and looked into her mouth, like a dentist. Her fangs were real, but shrank as she quivered in Penny's *nosferatu* grip. Red swirls dwindled in her eyes, and she was warm again, a frail thing.

Penny understood what the vampire boy was doing in the back room. At once, she was aghast and struck with admiration. She had heard of the warm temporarily taking on vampire attributes by drinking vampire blood without themselves being bitten. There was a story about Katie Reed and a flier in the First World War. But it was rare, and dangerous.

Well, it used to be rare.

All around her, mayfly vampires darted. A youth blundered into her arms and tried to bite her. She firmly pushed him away, breaking the fingers of his right hand to make a point. They would heal instantly, but ache like the Devil when he turned back into a real boy.

A worm of terror curled in her heart. To do such a thing meant having a vision. Vampires, made conservative by centuries, were rarely innovators. She was reminded, again, of Dracula, who had risen among the *nosferatu* by virtue of his willingness to venture into new, large-scale fields of conquest. Such vampires were always frightening.

Would it really be a good thing for Andy to meet this boy?

She saw the white jacket shining in the darkness. The vampire stood at the bar, with Steve Rubell, ringmaster of 54, and the movie actress Isabelle Adjani. Steve, as usual, was flying, hairstyle falling apart above his bald spot. His pockets bulged with petty cash, taken from the overstuffed tills.

Steve spotted her, understood her nod of interest, and signalled her to come over.

'Penny darling,' he said, 'look at me. I'm like you.'

He had fangs too. And red-smeared lips.

'I . . . am . . . a vampiah!'

For Steve, it was just a joke. There was a bitemark on Adjani's neck, which she dabbed with a bar napkin.

'This is just the biggest thing evah,' Steve said.

'Fabulous,' she agreed.

Her eyes fixed the vampire newcomer. He withstood her gaze. She judged him no longer a new-born but not yet an elder. He was definitely of the Dracula line.

'Introduce me,' she demanded, delicately.

Steve's red eyes focused.

'Andy is interested?'

Penny nodded. Whatever was swarming in his brain, Steve was sharp.

'Penelope, this is Johnny Pop. He's from Transylvania.'

'I am an American, now,' he said, with just a hint of accent.

'Johnny, my boy, this is the witch Penny Churchward.'

Penny extended her knuckles to be kissed. Johnny Pop took her fingers and bowed slightly, an old world habit.

'You cut quite a figure,' she said.

'You are an elder?'

'Good grief, no. I'm from the class of '88. One of the few survivors.'

'My compliments.'

He let her hand go. He had a tall drink on the bar, blood concentrate. He would need to get his blood count up, to judge by all his fluttering get.

Some fellow rose off the dance floor on ungainly, short-lived leather wings. He made it a few feet into the air, flapping furiously. Then there was a ripping and he collapsed onto the rest of the crowd, yelling and bleeding.

Johnny smiled and raised his glass to her.

She would have to think about this development.

'My friend Andy would like to meet you, Johnny.'

Steve was delighted, and slapped Johnny on the arm.

'Andy Warhol is the Vampire Queen of New York City,' he said. 'You have arrived, my deah!'

Johnny wasn't impressed. Or was trying hard not to be.

Politely, he said, 'Miss Churchward, I should like to meet your friend Mr Warhol.'

So, this ash-faced creature was coven master of New York. Johnny had seen Andy Warhol before, here and at the Mudd Club, and knew who he was, the man who painted soup cans and made the dirty movies. He hadn't known Warhol was a vampire, but now it was pointed out, it seemed obvious. What else could such a person be?

Warhol was not an elder but he was unreadable, beyond Johnny's experience. He would have to be careful, to pay proper homage to this master. It would not do to excite the enmity of the city's few other vampires: at least, not yet. Warhol's woman – consort? mistress? slave? – was intriguing, too. She danced on the edge of hostility, radiating prickly suspicion, but he had a hook of a kind in her too. Born to follow, she would trot after him as faithfully as she followed her artist master. He had met her kind before, stranded out of their time, trying to make a way in the world rather than reshape it to suit themselves. It would not do to underestimate her.

'Gee,' Warhol said, 'you must come to the Factory. There are things you could do.'

Johnny didn't doubt it.

Steve made a sign and a photographer appeared. Johnny noticed Penelope edging out of shot just before the flash went off. Andy, Steve and Johnny were caught in the bleached corner. Steve, grinning with his fresh teeth.

'Say, Johnny,' Steve said, 'we will show up, won't we? I mean, I've still got my image.'

Johnny shrugged. He had no idea whether the drac suck Steve had taken earlier would affect his reflection. That had as much to do with Nancy as him.

'Wait and see what develops,' Johnny said.

'If that's the way it has to be, that's the way it is.'

It didn't do to think too hard about what Americans said.

'Gee,' mused Andy, 'that's, uh, fa-antastic, that's a thought.'

Within months, Johnny would rule this city.

*

From 1964 to 1968, Andy abandoned painting – if silkscreen can be called that – in favour of film. Some have suggested that works like **Couch** (1964) or **The Thirteen Most Beautiful Boys** (1965) are just portraits that move; certainly, more people caught them as an ambient backdrop to the Exploding Plastic Inevitable than endured them reverentially at the Co-Op. **Movies**, not films, they were supposed to play to audiences too busy dancing or speeding or covering their bleeding ears to pay the sort of attention required by Hollywood narrative.

By now, 'Andy's vampire movies' had gone beyond standing joke – eight hours of the Empire State Building!! – and were taken seriously by genuine underground filmmakers like Stan Brakhage (who considered silent speed the stroke of genius). The Filmmakers' Co-Op regularly scheduled 'Warhol Festivals' and word got out that the films were, well, **dirty**, which – of course – pulled in audiences. **Suck-Job** was about as close to vampirism as even the most extreme New York audiences had seen, even if it was silent, black-and-white and slightly out of focus. Isabelle Dufresne, later the supervamp Ultra Violet, saw **Suck-Job** projected on a sheet at the Factory, and understood at once the strategy of incompletion, whereby the meat of the matter was beyond the frame. In **Dead for Fifteen Minutes: My Years With Andy Warhol** (1988), Ultra Violet writes: 'Although my eyes remain focused on the face of the young man receiving the suck job, my attention is constantly drawn to the empty space on the sheet below the screen. I am being visually assaulted and insulted at the same time. It is unnerving. I want to get up and seize the camera and focus it downward to capture the action. But I can't, and that's where the frustration comes in.'

Ultra Violet also reports that, during that screening, some Factory hangers-on present relieved the frustration by nibbling each other, drawing squeals of pain and streaks of quick-drying blood. Such tentative pretend-vampirism was common among the Mole People, the nighttime characters Andy gathered to help make 'his' movies and turned into his private coven in the back room of Max's Kansas City. With no genuine undead available, Andy made do with self-made supervamps, who showed up on film if not at rehearsals: Pope Ondine (who drew real blood), Brigid (Berlin) Polk, Baby Jane Hudson (who had once been a real-live movie star), Malanga's muse Mary Woronov, Carmillo Karnstein, Ingrid Supervamp. Brian Stableford would later coin the term 'lifestyle fantasists' for these people and their modern avatars, the goth murgatroyds. Like Andy, the Mole People already lived like vampires: shunning daylight, speeding all night, filing their teeth, developing pasty complexions, sampling each other's drug-laced blood.

The butcher's bill came in early. The dancer Freddie Herko, who appears in **Kiss** (1963) and **Dance Movie/Roller Skates** (1963), read in Montague Summers' **The Vampire: His Kith and Kin** (1928) that those who committed suicide spectacularly enough 'without fear' were reborn as 'powerful vampires'. Just before Halloween 1964, Herko danced across a friend's Greenwich Village apartment, trailing a ten-foot Batman/Dracula cloak, and sailed elegantly out of a fifth-floor window. Having skim-read the Summers and not bothered to form a Pact with the Devil, an essential part of the immortality-through-self-slaughter gambit, Herko did not rise from the dead. When he heard of Herko's defenestration, Warhol was almost irritated. 'Gee,' he sighed, 'why didn't he tell me he was going to do it?

We could have gone down there and filmed it.' Herko was just the first of the Warhol death cluster, his personal disaster series: Edie Sedgwick (1971), Tiger Morse (1972), Andrea Feldman (1972), Candy Darling (1974), Eric Emerson (1975), Gregory Battcock (1980), Tom Baker (1982), Jackie Curtis (1985), Valerie Solanas (1989), Ondine (1989). And Warhol himself (1968?). Only Andy made it back, of course. He had to be the vampire they all would have been, even Valerie.

*In 1965, the term 'vampire movies' took on another layer of meaning at the Factory, with the arrival of Ronald Tavel, a playwright hired to contribute situations (if not scripts) for the films, and Edie Sedgwick, a blueblood blonde who was, in many ways, Andy's ultimate supervamp. Movies like **The Death of Radu the Handsome** (1965), with Ondine as Vlad the Impaler's gay brother, and **Poor Little Dead Girl** (1965), with Edie as the Vampire Claudia, run seventy minutes (two uninterrupted thirty-five minute takes, the length of a film magazine, stuck together), have intermittently audible sound-tracks and mimic Hollywood to the extent of having something approaching narrative. Were it not for the incandescent person-alities of the supervamps, the beautiful and the damned, these efforts would be more like 'zombie movies', shambling gestures of mimesis, constantly tripping up as the immobile image (Andy had the most stoned Mole Person handle the camera) goes in and out of focus or the walk-on 'victims' run out of things to do and say. Ondine, Edie and a few others understand that the films are their own shot at vampire immortality. With dimestore plastic fangs and shrouds from the dress-up chest, these living beings cavort, preserved on film while their bodies are long in the grave, flickering in undeath. For Andy, the film camera,*

41

*like the silkscreen or the polaroid, was a vampire machine, a
process for turning life into frozen death, perfect and reproduci-
ble. Hurting people was always so interesting, and left the most
fabulous Rorschach stain patterns on the sheets.*

*Edie cut her hair to match Andy's wigs and took to wearing
imitations of his outfits, especially for photographs and openings. They looked like asexual twins or clones, but were really
trying to model themselves on that most terrifying denizen of
the world of darkness, the old vampire couple. R. D. Laing's
study **Helga and Heinrich** (1970) suggests that, after centuries
together, vampire couples mingle identities, sharing a conscious-
ness between two frail-seeming bodies, finishing each other's
sentences as the mind flickers between two skulls, moving in on
their victims in an instinctive pincer movement. If one partner
is destroyed, the other rots in sympathy. Edie would probably
have gone that far – she did eventually commit suicide – but
Andy was too self-contained to commit anything or commit to
anything. He saw her as the mirror he didn't like to look in –
his reflection reminded him that he was alive, after all – and
would often play the mimic game, patterned after Harpo Marx,
with her, triumphantly squirting milk from his mouth or
producing a walnut from a fist to show he was the original and
she the copy. When he said he wanted everyone to be alike, he
was expressing a solipsist not an egalitarian ideal: everyone
was to be like him, but he was still to be the mould.*

   Conklin, *ibid*

He fed often now, less for sustenance than for business.
This one, seized just before sunrise, was the last of three
taken throughout a single April night. He had waylaid

the Greek girl, a seamstress in the garment district, on her way to a long day's work. She was too terrified to make a sound as Johnny ripped into her throat. Blood poured into his gaping mouth, and he swallowed. He fed his lust, his need. It wasn't just blood, it was money.

The girl, dragged off the street into an alley, had huge, startled eyes. Her ghost was in him as he bled her. She was called Thana, Death. The name stuck in his craw, clogging the lizard stem of his brain that always came alive as he fed. She should have been called Zoë, Life. Was something wrong with her blood? She had no drugs, no disease, no madness. She started to fight him, mentally. The girl knew about her ghost, could struggle with him on a plane beyond the physical. Her unexpected skill shocked him.

He broke the bloody communion and dropped her onto some cardboard boxes. He was exhilarated and terrified. Thana's ghost snapped out of his mind and fell back into her. She sobbed soundlessly, mouth agape.

'Death,' he said, exorcising her.

Her blood made him full to the point of bursting. The swollen veins around his mouth and neck throbbed like painful erections. Just after a big feed, he was unattractively jowly, turgid sacs under his jawline, purplish flush to his cheeks and chest. He couldn't completely close his mouth, crowded as it was with blocky, jagged fangs.

He thought about wasting Thana, fulfilling the prophecy of her name.

No. He must not kill while feeding. Johnny was taking more victims but drinking less from each, holding back from killing. If people had to be killed, he'd do it without taking blood, much as it went against the Father's warrior instinct that subjugation of the vanquished should be commemorated at least by a mouthful of hot blood. This was America and things were different.

Who'd have thought there'd be such a fuss about Nancy and Sid? He was surprised by the extensive news coverage of another drab death at the Chelsea. Sid, a slave who could never finger Johnny without burning out his brain completely, was charged with murder. Out on bail, he was remanded back to jail for bottling Patti Smith's brother. On Riker's Island, he found out 'punk' had another meaning in prison. Kicked loose again, he had turned up dead of an overdose, with a suntan that struck witnesses as being unusual for February. It was either down to the political situation in Iran or Johnny's own enterprise: in the weeks Sid was locked up and kicking, heroin had become infinitely purer, perhaps thanks to Persians getting their money out in drugs, perhaps dealers competing with drac. Because Sid was well-known, the ragged end of his life was picked apart by a continuing police investigation. Loose ends could turn up; someone like Rockets Redglare, who had dealt in Room 100, might remember seeing Sid and Nancy with a vampire on the night of the killing. Johnny had no idea a singer who couldn't sing would be so famous. Even Andy was impressed by the headlines, and wondered whether he should do a Sid picture to catch the moment.

He knelt by Thana, holding her scarf to her throat

wound. He took her hand and put it up to the makeshift dressing, indicating where she should press. In her hating eyes, he had no reflection. To her, he was nothing.

Fine.

Johnny left the girl and looked for a cab.

He had a penthouse apartment now, rent paid in cash every month, at the Bramford, a Victorian brownstone of some reputation. A good address was important. He needed somewhere to keep his clothes, and a coffin lined with Transylvanian dirt. At heart, Johnny was a traditionalist. Andy was the same, prizing American antique furniture – American antique, hah! – and art deco bric-a-brac, filling his town house with the prizes of the past while throwing out the art of the future in his Factory.

Johnny had over $11,500,000 in several accounts, and cash stashes in safe deposit boxes all over the city. He intended to pay income taxes on some of it, quite soon. In a moment of candour, he had discussed his business with the Churchward woman. She was the only vampire of real experience in the city, besides Andy – who clammed up shut when asked about feeding, though Johnny knew he took nips from all his assistants. Johnny and Penelope couldn't decide whether what he did was against the law or not, but judged it best to keep quiet. Selling his own blood was a legal grey area, but assault and murder weren't. He was reluctant to relinquish those tools entirely, but accepted that standards of behaviour in America were ostensibly different from those of his European backwater homeland. It wasn't that assault and murder were less common here than in Romania, but the authorities made more noise about it.

Those like Thana, left alive after his caresses, might argue that his powers of fascination constituted coercion, that he had perpetrated upon them a form of rape or robbery. Statutes against organ-snatching might even be applicable. Penelope said that soon it wouldn't be safe to pick up a Mr Goodbar and suck him silly without getting a signature on a consent form.

The first real attempt to destroy him had came not from the church or the law, but from criminals. He was cutting into their smack and coke action. A couple of oddly dressed black men came for him with silver razors. The iron of the Father rose up within him and he killed them both, shredding their clothes and faces to make a point. He found out their names from the *Daily Bugle*, Youngblood Priest and Tommy Gibbs. He wondered if the black men he had seen outside the Chelsea on the night he met Andy were in with that Harlem crowd. He had glimpsed them again, several times, singly and as a pair. They were virtual twins, though one was further into the dark then the other. The knifeman's partner packed a crossbow under his coat. They would not be so easy to face down.

The Mott Street Triads had found a vampire of their own – one of those hopping Mandarins, bound by prayers pasted to his forehead – and tried feeding and milking him, cooking their own drac. Markedly inferior, their product was exhausted within a month, an entire body gone to dust and sold on the street. Soon such *nosferatu* slaves, captured and used up fast, would be common. Other vampires would sell their own drac, in America or their homelands. If the craze could take off in New York, then it would eventually trickle down to everywhere.

Johnny had repeatedly turned down offers of 'partnership' from the established suppliers of drugs. A cash payment of $6,000,000 to the Prizzi Family eliminated most of the hassle his people had been getting on the street. The Harlem rogues were off his case. He could pass for Italian, which meant he was to be respected for the moment. Mafia elders like Corrado Prizzi and Michael Corleone were men of rough honour; younger wiseguys like John Gotti and Frank White, on the rise even as the dons were fading, were of a different stripe. Gotti, or someone like him, would eventually move into drac. By then, Johnny intended to be retired and in another city.

The cops were interested. He had spotted them at once, casually loitering around crime scenes, chatting with dazed witnesses, giving penetrating stares. He had them marked down: the bogus hippie with the woolly vest, the completely bald man with the good suit, the maniac driver in the battered porkpie hat. Like the Father, he knew when to be careful, when to be daring. The police meant nothing in this land. They didn't even have silver bullets, like *Securitate* in the Old Country.

His own children – the dhampires – were busy. With his blood in them, they changed for a while. The first few times, they just relished the new senses, the feel of fangs in their mouths, the quickening of reflexes. Then, red thirst pricked. They needed to assuage it, before the suck wore off.

Apparently, the biting had started in the semi-underground gay clubs, among the leather-and-chains community. Johnny guessed one of the Studio 54 bouncers was the fountainhead. Both Burns and Stu were denizens of those cruising places. Within a few months, the biting had got out of hand. Every week, there were deaths, as dhampires lost control during the red rush, took too much from their lovers of the moment.

The money, however, kept coming in.

In the lobby, already brightening with dawnlight, an unnerving twelve-year-old clacked together two pink perspex eggs on a string. Johnny understood he was trying to get into the *Guinness Book of Records*. The child was a holy terror, allowed to run loose by his indulgent parents and their adoring circle. More than one resident of the Bramford had expressed a desire to be around when little Adrian Woodhouse 'got his come-uppance', but Johnny knew it would not do to cross the boy. If you intend to live forever, do not make enemies of children.

He hurried towards the cage elevator, intent on getting out of ear-range of the aural water torture.

'Johnny, Johnny . . .'

As he spun around, excess blood dizzied him. He felt it sloshing around inside. Everything was full: his stomach, his heart, his veins, his bladder, his lungs. It was practically backing up to his eyeballs.

The dhampire was cringing in a shrinking shadow.

'Johnny,' she said, stepping into the light.

Her skin darkened and creased, but she ignored it. She had crumpled bills in her hand, dirty money. He could imagine what she had done to get it.

It was the girl he had once called Nocturna. The Virgin of 54. She wasn't fresh any more, in any way.

'Please,' she begged, mouth open and raw.

'Things have changed,' he said, stepping into the elevator, drawing the mesh across between them. He saw her red-rimmed eyes.

'Take it,' she said, rolling the bills into tubes and shoving them through the grille. They fell at his feet.

'Talk to Rudy or Elvira,' he said. 'They'll fix you up with a suck.'

She shook her head, desperately. Her hair was a mess, singed white in patches. She grabbed the grille, fingers sticking through like worms.

'I don't want a suck, I want *you*.'

'You don't want me, darling. You can't afford me. Now, pull in your claws or you'll lose them.'

She was crying rusty tears.

He wrenched the lever and the elevator began to rise. The girl pulled her hands free. Her face sank and disappeared. She had pestered him before. He would have to do something about her.

It wasn't that he didn't do business that way any more,

but that he had to be more selective about the clientele. For the briefest of suckles from the vein, the price was now $10,000. He was choosy about the mouths he spurted into.

Everyone else could just buy a suck.

Rudy and Elvira were waiting in the foyer of the apartment, red-eyed from the night, coming down slowly. They were dhampires themselves, of course. The Father had known the worth of warm slaves, his gypsies and madmen, and Johnny had taken some care in selecting the vassals he needed. As Johnny entered the apartment, peeling off his floor-length turquoise swede coat and tossing away his black-feathered white Stetson hat, Rudy leaped up from the couch almost to attention. Elvira, constricted inside a black sheath dress low-necked enough to show her navel, raised a welcoming eyebrow and tossed aside *The Sensuous Woman*. Rudy took his coat and hat and hung them up. Elvira rose like a snake from a basket and air-kissed his cheeks. She touched black nails to his face, feeling the bloat of the blood.

They proceeded to the dining room.

Rudy Pasko, a hustler Johnny had picked up on the A-train, dreamed of turning, becoming like his master. Jittery, nakedly ambitious, *American*, he would be a real monster, paying everybody back for ignoring him in life. Johnny wasn't comfortable with Rudy's focused needs, but, for the moment, he had his uses.

Elvira, this year's compleat Drac Hag, was a better bet for immortality. She knew when to run cool or hot, and took care to keep a part of herself back, even while snuffing mountains of drac and chewing on any youth who happened to be passing. She liked to snack on gay men, claiming – with her usual dreadful wordplay – that they had better taste than straights. Andy had passed her on, from the Factory.

The money was on the polished oak dining table, in attaché cases. It had already been counted, but Johnny sat down and did it again. Rudy called him 'the Count', almost mockingly. The boy didn't understand, the money wasn't Johnny's until it was counted. The obsessive-compulsive thing was a trick of the Dracula bloodline. Some degenerate, mountain-dwelling distant cousins could be distracted from their prey by a handful of pumpkin seeds, unable to pass by without counting every one. That was absurd, this was important. Andy understood about money, why it was essential, not for what it could buy, but in itself. Numbers were beautiful.

Johnny's fingers were so sensitive that he could make the count just by riffling the bundles, by caressing the cash. He picked out the dirty bills, the torn or taped or stained notes, and tossed them to Rudy.

There was $158,591 on the table, a fair night's taking. His personal rake would be an even $100,000.

'Where does the ninety-one dollars come from, Rudy?'

The shrugged. The non-negotiable price of a suck was $500. There shouldn't be looser change floating around.

'Boys and girls have expenses,' Rudy said.

'They are not to dip into the till,' Johnny said, using an expression he had recently learned. 'They are to hand

over the taking. If they have expenses, they must ask
you to cover them. You have enough for all eventualities,
have you not?'

Rudy looked at the heap of messy bills and nodded. He
had to be reminded of his hook sometimes.

'Now, things must be taken care of.'

Rudy followed him into the reception room. The heart
of the penthouse, the reception room was windowless
but with an expanse of glass ceiling. Just now, with the
sun rising, the skylight was curtained by a rolling metal
blind drawn by a hand-cranked winch.

There was no furniture, and the hardwood floor was
protected by a plastic sheet. It was Rudy's duty to get the
room ready for Johnny by dawn. He had laid out shallow
metal trays in rows, like seed-beds in a nursery.

Johnny undid his fly and carefully pissed blood onto
the first tray. The pool spread, until it lapped against the
sides. He paused his flow, and proceeded to the next
tray, and the next. In all, he filled thirty-seven trays to a
depth of about a quarter of an inch. He lost his bloat,
face smoothing and tightening, clothes hanging properly
again.

Johnny watched from the doorway as Rudy worked
the winch, rolling the blind. Rays of light speared down
through the glass ceiling, falling heavily on the trays.
Morning sun was the best, the purest. The trays smoked
slightly, like vats of tomato soup on griddles. There was
a smell he found offensive, but which the warm – even
dhampires – could not distinguish. Like an elder exposed
to merciless daylight, the blood was turning to granulated

material. Within a few hours, it would all be red dust, like the sands of Mars. Drac.

In the afternoon, as he slept in his white satin-lined coffin, a troop of good Catholic boys whose fear of Johnny was stronger than the bloodhooks in their brains came to the apartment and, under Elvira's supervision, worked on the trays, scooping up and measuring out the powdered blood into foil twists ('sucks' or 'jabs') that retailed for $500 each. After sunset, the boys (and a few girls) took care of the distribution, spreading out to the clubs and parties and street corners and park nooks where the dhampires hung out.

Known on the street as drac or bat's blood, the powder could be snuffed, swallowed, smoked or heated to liquid and injected. With a fresh user, the effect lasted the hours of the night and was burned out of the system at sunrise. After a few weeks, the customer was properly hooked, a dhampire, and needed three or four sucks a night to keep sharp. No one knew about long-term effects yet, though serious dhampires like Nocturna were prone to severe sunburn and even showed signs of being susceptible to spontaneous combustion. Besides a red thirst for a gulp or two of blood, the dhampire also had a need, of course, to raise cash to feed the habit. Johnny didn't care much about that side of the business, but the *Daily Bugle* had run editorials about the rise in mugging, small burglary, car crime and other petty fund-raising activities.

Thus far, Johnny was sole supplier of the quality stuff.

During their short-lived venture, the Triads had cut their dwindling drac with cayenne pepper, tomato paste and powdered catshit. The Good Catholics were all dhampires themselves, though he kicked them out and cut them off if they exceeded their prescribed dosage – which kept them scrupulously honest about cash. His major expenses were kickbacks to the Families, club owners, bouncers, street cops and other mildly interested parties.

Johnny Pop would be out of the business soon. He was greedy for more than money. Andy had impressed on him the importance of being famous.

*Warhol and Tavel made **Veneer** (1965), the first film version of Bram Stoker's **Dracula** (1897). In **Stargazer: Ady Warhol's World and His Films** (1973), Stephen Kock reports: 'Warhol handed Tavel a copy of the novel with the remark that it might be easier to compose a scenario based on fiction than one spun out of pure fantasy. He had acquired the rights to the Stoker book for $3,000, he said; it ought to make a good movie. And so it did. It's not hard to guess why Warhol was impressed by **Dracula**. (I should mention in passing that, contrary to the myth he propagates, Warhol is quite widely read.) The book is filled with the sexuality of violence; it features a tough, erotic vampire dandy joyously dominating a gang of freaks; its theme is humiliation within a world that is simultaneously sordid and unreal; it is a history which at once did and did not happen, a purposeful lie. Finally, there is the question of class . . . I think Warhol participates very deeply in America's best-kept secret – the painful, deeply denied intensity with which we* *experience our class structure. We should not forget that we are speaking of the son of semiliterate immigrants, whose father was a steelworker in Pittsburgh. Within the terms of his own intensely specialised mentality, Warhol has lived through American class humiliation and American poverty. And **Dracula**, although British, is very much about the sexuality of social class as it merges with spiritual domination.'*

Casting Edie as an ephebic silver-haired Dracula (Drella, indeed), Gerard Malanga as a whip-wielding but humiliated Harker and Ondine as a sly Van Helsing, Warhol populated the Factory's Transylvania and Carfax Abbey (the same 'set', black sheets hung with silver cobwebs) with lost souls. Well before Francis Ford Coppola, Warhol saw that the problems in filming the novel could be side-stepped by force of will. Indeed, he approached the enterprise with a deliberate diffidence that all but ensured this would not be a 'proper' film. Ronnie Tavel at least read half the book before getting bored and typing out a script in his usual three days. Since shooting consisted of a complete run-through of the script as a performance, with breaks only when the magazine ran out, Tavel considered that there ought to be actual rehearsals and that the actors should stoop to learning their lines. Too fearful of confrontation to disagree, Warhol simply sabotaged the rehearsals Tavel organised and even the shooting of the film by inviting the Press and various parasites to the Factory to observe and interfere, and sending Malanga off on trivial errands or keeping him up until dawn at parties to prevent him from even reading the script (as in the book, Harker has the most to say). Koch, again: *'The sense that making a film was work – that it should involve the concentrated attention of work – was utterly banished, and on shooting day the Factory merely played host to another "Scene", another party.'*

Stoker's intricate plot is reduced to situations. Harker, in black leather pants and Victorian deerstalker, visits Castle Dracula, carrying a crucifix loaned to the production by Andy's mother, and is entertained, seduced and assaulted by the Count (Edie's enormous fangs keep slipping out of her mouth) and his three gesticulating vampire brides (Marie Mencken, Carmillo Karnstein, International Velvet). Later, in Carfax Abbey, Harker – roped to the Factory Couch – watches as Dracula fascinates and vampirises Mina (Mary Woronov) in a tango that climaxes with Mina drinking Campbell's Tomato Soup from a can Dracula has opened with a thumb-talon and which he declares is his vampire blood. Van Helsing appears, with his fearless vampire hunters – Lord Godalming (Chuck Wein), Quincey Morris (Joe Dallesandro), Dr Seward (Paul America) – dragged by Renfield (a young, ravaged Lou Reed), who is leashed like a bloodhound.

Crucifixes, stakes, whips and communion wafers are tossed back and forth in a bit of knockabout that makes some of the cast giggle uncontrollably and drives others – notably, the still-tethered Malanga – to furious distraction. In Tavel's script, as in Stoker's novel, Van Helsing's band corner and destroy Dracula, who was to be spray-painted silver and suffocated, but Ondine is distracted when a girl who happens to be on the couch for no real reason – she seems to be a set-visitor straying into frame – calls him a 'phony', and Ondine ignores the King Vampire to lash out at this impertinent chit, going for her face with his false fingernails. Ondine's methadrine rant rises in a *crescendo, peaks and fades: 'May God forgive you, you're a phony, Little Miss Phony, you're a disgusting phony, get off this set, you're a disgrace to humanity, you're a disgrace to yourself, you're a loathsome fool, your husband's a loathsome fool . . . I'm sorry, I just can't go on, this is just too much, I don't want to go on.' The camera, handled this time by Bud Wirtschafter, tries to follow the unexpected action, and for a few brief frames catches the ghost-white face of Andy himself hanging shocked in the gloom; the removal of this slip is perhaps the only proper edit in any Warhol film made before the arrival of Paul Morrissey. Van Helsing, inconsolable, stands alone and the film runs on and on, as he reassembles himself.*

*Edie, fangs spat out but still regally and perfectly Dracula, gets Wirtschafter's attention by tossing the soup can at him, spattering the lens, and commands the frame, hands on hips, for a few seconds before the film runs out. 'I am Dracula,' she insists, the only line of dialogue taken directly (if unintentionally) from the book. 'I **am** Dracula,' she repeats, sure of herself for the last time in her life. Stoker had intended to inflict upon Dracula the defeat he eluded in reality, but Edie has dragged Warhol's Dracula movie back to the truth. In the Factory, Drella bests the squabbling Vampire Slayers and reigns forever.*

   Conklin, *ibid*

Johnny Pop was certainly the social success of the Summer. He had just showed up at Trader Vic's with *Margaret Trudeau* on his elegant arm. Penelope was not surprised, and Andy was silently ecstatic. An inveterate collector of people, he delighted in the idea of the Transylvanian hustler and the Prime Minister's ex getting together.

Margaux Hemingway would be furious; she had confided in Andy and Penny that she thought it was serious with Johnny. Penny could have told her what was serious with Johnny, but she didn't think any warm woman would understand.

From across the room, as everyone turned to look at the couple, Penny observed Johnny, realising why no one else saw him as she did. He had Olde Worlde charm by the bucketful, and that thirsty edge that had made him seem a rough beast was gone. His hair was an improbable construction, teased and puffed every which way, and his lips were a girl's. But his eyes were Dracula's. It had taken her a while to notice, for she had really known *il principe* only after his fire had dwindled. This was what the *young* Dracula, freshly *nosferatu*, must have been like. This was the bat-cloaked creature of velvet night who with sheer smoking magnetism had overwhelmed flighty Lucy, virtuous Mina and stately Victoria, who had bested Van Helsing and stolen an empire. He didn't dance so often now that he had the city's attention, but all his moves were like dancing, his gestures so considered, his looks so perfect.

He had told several versions of the story, but always insisted he was Dracula's get, perhaps the last to be turned personally by the King Vampire in his five-hundred-year reign. Johnny didn't like to give dates, but Penny put his conversion at somewhere before the Last War. Who he had been when warm was another matter. He claimed to be a lineal descendant as well as get, the last modern son of some byblow of the Impaler, which was why the dying bloodline had fired in him, making him the true Son of Dracula. She could almost believe it. Though he was proud to name his Father-in-Darkness, he didn't like to talk about the Old Country and what had brought him to America. There were stories there, she would wager. Eventually, it would all come out. He had probably drained a commissar's daughter and got out one step ahead of red vampire killers.

There was trouble in the Carpathians now. The Transylvania Movement, wanting to claim Dracula's ancient fiefdom as a homeland for all the displaced vampires of the world, were in open conflict with Ceausescu's army. The only thing Johnny had said about that mess was that he would prefer to be in America than Romania. After all, the modern history of vampirism – so despised by the Transylvanians – had begun when Dracula left his homelands for what was in 1885 the most exciting, modern city in the world. She conceded the point: Johnny Pop was displaying the real Dracula spirit, not TM reactionaries like Baron Meinster and Anton Crainic who wanted to retreat to their castles and pretend it was still the Middle Ages.

Andy got fidgety as Johnny worked the room, greeting poor Truman Capote or venerable Paulette Goddard, sharp Ivan Boesky or needy Liza Minnelli. He was deliberately delaying his inevitable path to Andy's table. It was like a Renaissance court, Penny realised. Eternal shifts of power and privilege, of favour and slight. Three months ago, Johnny had needed to be in with Andy; now, Johnny had risen to such a position that he could

afford to hold himself apart, to declare independence.
She had never seen Andy on the hook this badly, and
was willing to admit she took some delight in it. At last,
the master was mastered.

Eventually, Johnny arrived and displayed his prize.

Penny shook Mrs Trudeau's hand and felt the chill
coming from her. Her scarlet choker didn't quite match
her crimson evening dress. Penny could smell the musk
of her scabs.

Johnny was drinking well, these nights.

Andy and Johnny sat together, close. Neither had
anything interesting to say, which was perhaps why they
needed so many people around them.

Mrs Trudeau frowned, showing her own streak of
jealousy. Penny wouldn't be able to explain to her what
Andy and Johnny had, why everyone else was superflu-
ous when they were together. Despite the fluctuations in
their relationship, they were one being with two bodies.
Without saying much, Johnny made Andy choke with
laughter he could never let out. There was a reddish
flush to Andy's albino face.

'Don't mind them,' Penny told Mrs Trudeau. 'They're
bats.'

'I don't suppose this'd do anything for you,' said the girl
from *Star Wars* whose real name Penny had forgotten,
cutting a line of red powder on the coffee table with a
silver razorblade.

Penny shrugged.

Vampires did bite each other. If one were wounded

almost to death, an infusion of another's *nosferatu* blood could have restorative powers. Blood would be offered by an inferior undead to a coven master to demonstrate loyalty. Penny had no idea what, if any, effect drac would have on her and wasn't especially keen on finding out. The scene was pretty much a bore.

Princess Leia was evidently a practised dhampire. She snorted through a tubed $100 bill and held her head back. Her eyes reddened and her teeth grew points.

'Arm wrestle?' she asked.

Penny wasn't interested. Dhampires all had this rush of vampire power but no real idea of what to do with it. Except nibble. They didn't even feed properly.

Most of the people at this party were drac addicts. They went for the whole bit, black capes and fingerless black widow web gloves, Victorian cameos at the throat, lots of velvet and leather, puffy minidresses over thigh-boots.

Half this lot had dracced themselves up completely for a midnight screening of *The Rocky Horror Picture Show* at the Waverly, and were just coming down, which meant they were going around the room, pestering anyone they thought might be holding out on a stash, desperate to get back up there. There was a miasma of free-floating paranoia, which Penny couldn't keep out of her head.

'Wait 'til this gets to the Coast,' said Princess Leia. 'It'll be monstrous.'

Penny had to agree.

She had lost Andy and Johnny at CBGB's, and fallen in with this crowd. The penthouse apartment apparently belonged to some political big-wig she had never heard of, Hal Philip Walker, but he was out of town and Brooke Hayward was staying here with Dennis Hopper. Penny had the idea that Johnny knew Hopper from some foreign debauch, and wanted to avoid him – which, if true, was unusual.

She was welcome here, she realised, because she was a vampire.

It hit her that if the drac ran out, there was a direct source in the room. She was stronger than any warm person, but it was a long time since she had fought anyone. The sheer press of dhampires would tell. They could hold her down and cut her open, then suck her dry, leaving her like crushed orange pulp. For the first time since turning, she understood the fear the warm had of her kind. Johnny had changed things permanently.

Princess Leia, fanged and clawed, eyed her neck slyly, and reached out to touch her.

'Excuse me,' said Penny, slipping away.

Voices burbled in her mind. She was on a wavelength with all these dhampires, who didn't know how to communicate. It was just background chatter, amplified to skull-cracking levels.

In the bedroom where she had left her coat, a Play-mate of the Month and some rock 'n' roll guy were messily performing dhampire 69, gulping from wounds in each other's wrists. She had fed earlier, and the blood did nothing for her.

A Broadway director tried to talk to her.

Yes, she had seen *Pacific Overtures*. No, she didn't want to invest in *Sweeney Todd*.

Where had anybody got the idea that she was rich?

That fat Albanian from *Animal House*, fangs like sharpened cashew nuts, claimed newfound vampire skills had helped him solve Rubik's cube. He wore a black Inverness cape over baggy Y-fronts. His eyes flashed red and gold like a cat's in headlights.

Penny had a headache.

She took the elevator down to the street.

While looking for a cab, she was accosted by some dreadful drac hag. It was the girl Johnny called Nocturna, now a snowy-haired fright with yellow eyes and rotten teeth.

The creature pressed money on her, a crumpled mess of notes.

'Just a suck, precious,' she begged.

Penny was sickened.

The money fell from the dhampire's hands, and was swept into the gutter.

'I think you'd better go home, dear,' advised Penny.

'Just a suck.'

Nocturna laid a hand on her shoulder, surprisingly strong. She retained some *nosferatu* attributes.

'Johnny still loves me,' she said, 'but he has business to take care of. He can't fit me in, you see. But I need a suck, just a little kiss, nothing serious.'

Penny took Nocturna's wrist but couldn't break the hold.

The dhampire's eyes were yolk yellow, with shots of blood. Her breath was foul. Her clothes, once fashionable, were ragged and gamey.

Penny glanced up and down the street. She could use a cop, or Spider-Man. People were passing, but in the distance. No one noticed this little scene.

Nocturna brought out something from her reticule. A Stanley knife. Penny felt a cold chill as the blade touched her cheek, then a venomous sting. The tool was silvered. She gasped in pain, and the dhampire stuck her mouth over the cut.

Penny struggled, but the dhampire was suddenly strong, juiced up by pure drac. She would make more cuts and take more sucks.

'You're his friend,' Nocturna said, lips red. 'He won't mind. I'm not being unfaithful.'

Penny supposed she deserved this.

But as the red rush dazed Nocturna, Penny broke free of the dhampire. She dabbed her cheek. Because of the silver, the cut would stay open, perhaps even leave a scar. Penny had too many of those, but this one would be where it showed.

There were people nearby, watching. Penny saw their red eyes. More dhampires, out for drac, out for her blood. She backed towards the lobby, cursing Johnny Pop.

Nocturna staggered after her.

A taxi cab stormed down the street, scattering dhampires. Penny stuck out her hand and flagged it down. Nocturna howled, and flew at her. Penny wrenched open the cab door and threw herself in. She told the driver to drive off, anywhere, fast.

Nocturna and the others hissed at the window, nails scratching the glass.

The cab sped up and left them behind.

Penny was resolved. Penance was one thing, but enough was enough. She would get out of this city. The Factory could run itself. She would leave Andy to Johnny, and hope they were satisfied with each other.

'Someday a rain's gonna come,' said the taxi driver. 'And wash the scum off the streets.'

She wished she could agree with him.

It is easy to overstate the importance of Nico to Warhol's late '60s work. She was, after all, his first 'real' vampire. Croaking, German and blonde, she was the dead image of Edie, and thus of Andy. Nico Otzak, turned some time in the '50s, arrived in New York in 1965, with her doll-like get Ari, and presented her card at the Factory. She trailed the very faintest of associations with Dracula himself, having been a fringe member of that last party, in Rome 1959, which climaxed in the true death of the Vampire King. 'She was myterious and European,' Andy said, abstaining from any mention of the v word, 'a real moon goddess type.' Like Dracula, she gave the impression of having used up the Old Worlde and moved on, searching for 'a young country, full of blood'.

*In **Edie: An American Biography** (1982), Jean Stein definitely refutes the popular version, in which the naïve, warm American is supplanted by the cold, dead European. Edie*

Sedgwick was on the point of turning from vampire to victim before Nico's arrival; she had made the cardinal error of thinking herself indispensable, a real star, and Andy was silently irked by her increasing need for publicity as herself rather than as his mirror. She had already strayed from the Factory and towards the circle of Bob Dylan, tempted by more serious drug habits and heterosexuality. Edie was justifiably miffed that the limited financial success of the films benefited only Andy; his position was that she was rich anyway – 'an heiress', one of his favourite words – and didn't need the money, though far less well-off folk did as much or more work on the films and silkscreens for similarly derisory pay. Edie's self-destruction cannot be laid entirely on Andy and Nico – the Dylan crowd hardly helped, moving her up from amphetamines to heroin – but it is undeniably true that without Warhol, Edie would never have become, in the English expression, 'dead famous'.

With Nico, Andy finally had his vampire. At the back of their association must have been the possibility – the promise? – that she would turn him, but for the moment, Andy held back. To become someone's get would have displaced him from the centre of his life, and that was insupportable. When he turned, a circumstance that remains mysterious, he would do so through anonymous blood donation, making himself – as usual – his own get, his own creature. Besides, no one could seriously want Nico for a mother-in-darkness; for the rest of her nights, she drew blood from Ari, her own get, and this vampire incest contributed to the rot that would destroy them both.

Andy was especially fascinated by Nico's relationship with *mirrors and film. She was one of those vampires who have no reflection, though he did his best to turn her into a creature who was all reflection with no self. He had her sing 'I'll Be Your Mirror', for instance. 'High Ashbury', the oddest segment of ****/**Twenty Four Hour Movie** (1966), places Ondine and Ultra Violet either side of an absence, engaged in conversation with what seems to be a disembodied voice. There are signs of Nico's physical presence during the shoot: the displacement of cushions, a cigarette that darts like a hovering dragonfly, a puff of smoke outlining an oesophagus. But the vampire woman just isn't there. That may be the point. Andy took photographs of silver-foiled walls and untenanted chairs and passed them off as portraits of Nico. He even silkscreened an empty coffin for an album cover.*

*Having found his vampire muse, Andy had to do **something** with her, so he stuck her together with the Velvet Underground – a band who certainly weren't that interested in having a girl singer who drank human blood – as part of the Exploding Plastic Inevitable, the club events he staged at the Dom on St Mark's Place in 1966. Amidst so much black leather, he dressed Nico in bone-white and put an angelic spotlight on her, especially when she wasn't singing. Lou Reed bought a crucifix, and started looking for a way out. The success of the EPI may well have been partially down to a wide cross-section of New Yorkers who were intrigued by Nico; most Americans in 1966 had never been in a room with a vampire, a real vampire. Andy knew that and made sure that, no matter how conveniently dark the rest of the packed club was, Nico was always visible, always the red-eyed wraith murmuring her way* *through 'Femme Fatale' without taking a breath. That song, of course, is a promise and a threat: 'think of her at nights, feel the way she bites . . .'*

As the Velvets performed, Warhol hid in the rafters like the Phantom of the Opera, working the lights and the projectors, cranking up the sound. Like Ulysses, he filled his ears with wax to get through the night. Behind the band, he screened his films. Often, as his real vampire paraded herself, he would show **Veneer**, *trying to project Edie onto Nico as he projected himself upon them both.*

Everybody agrees: between 1966 and 1968, Andy Warhol was a monster.

Conklin, *ibid*

Johnny was one of the privileged few allowed into Andy's town house to witness the artist's levée. At high summer, it was impractical to wait for sundown before venturing out – so Johnny had to be ferried the short distance from the Bramford to East 66th St in a sleek limo with polaroid windows and hustled under a parasol up to the door of Number 57.

With the Churchward woman's desertion, there was a blip in the smooth running of Andy's social life and he was casting around for a replacement Girl of the Year. Johnny was wary of being impressed into taking too many of Penny Penitent's duties. There were already so many demands on his time, especially with that mad Bella Abzug whipping the NYPD into a frenzy about 'the drac problem'. It wasn't even illegal yet, but his dealers were rousted every night, and his pay-offs to the Families and the cops ratcheted up every week, which pushed him to raise the price of a suck, which meant that dhamps had to peddle more ass or bust more head to scrape together the cash they needed. The papers were full of vampire murders, and real vampires weren't even suspects.

The two-storey lobby of Number 57 was dominated by imperial busts – Napoleon, Caesar, Dracula – and still-packed crates of sculptures and paintings. Things were everywhere, collected but uncatalogued, most still in the original wrapping.

Johnny sat on an upholstered chaise longue and leafed through a male pornographic magazine that was on top of a pile of periodicals that stretched from *The New York Review of Books* to *The Fantastic Four*. He heard Andy moving about upstairs, and glanced at the top of the wide staircase. Andy made an entrance, a skull-faced spook-mask atop a floor-length red velvet dressing gown which dragged behind him as he descended, like Scarlett O'Hara's train.

In this small, private moment – with no one else around to see – Andy allowed himself to smile, a terminally ill little boy indulging his love of dressing-up. It wasn't just that Andy was a poseur, but that he let everyone know it and still found the reality in the fakery, making the posing the point. When Andy pretended, he just showed up the half-hearted way everyone else did the same thing. In the months he had been in New York, Johnny had learned that being an American was just like being a vampire, to feed off the dead and to go on and

on and on, making a virtue of unoriginality, waxing a
corpse-face to beauty. In a country of surfaces, no one
cared about the rot that lay beneath the smile, the shine
and the dollar. After the persecutions of Europe, it was
an enormous relief.

Andy extended a long-nailed hand at an occasional
table by the chaise longue. It was heaped with the night's
invitations, more parties and openings and galas than
even Andy could hit before dawn.

'Choose,' he said.

Johnny took a handful of cards, and summarised them
for Andy's approval or rejection. Shakespeare in the Park,
Paul Toombs in *Timon of Athens* ('gee, misa-anthropy'). A
charity ball for some new wasting disease ('gee, sa-ad').
An Anders Wolleck exhibit of metal sculptures ('gee, fa-
abulous'). A premiere for the latest Steven Spielberg film
1941 ('gee, wo-onderful'). A screening at Max's Kansas
City of a work in progress by Scott and Beth B, starring
Lydia Lunch and Teenage Jesus ('gee, u-underground').
A night-club act by Divine ('gee, na-aughty'). Parties by
and for John Lennon, Tony Perkins ('ugh *Psycho*'), Rich-
ard Hell and Tom Verlaine, Jonathan and Jennifer Hart
('ick!'), Blondie ('the cartoon character or the band?'),
Malcolm McLaren ('be-est not'), David JoHansen, Edgar
Allan Poe ('ne-ever-more'), Frank Sinatra ('Old Hat Rat
Pack Hack!').

The night had some possibilities.

Andy was in a sulk. Truman Capote, lisping through silly
fangs, had spitefully told him about an Alexander Cock-

burn parody, modelled on the lunch chatter of Warhol and Colacello with Imelda Marcos as transcribed in *Inter/VIEW*. Andy, of course, had to sit down in the middle of the party and pore through the piece. In Cockburn's version, Bob and Andy took Count Dracula to supper at Mortimer's Restaurant on the Upper East Side and prodded him with questions like 'Don't you wish you'd been able to spend Christmas in Transylvania?' and 'Is there still pressure on you to think of your image and act a certain way?'

Johnny understood the real reason that the supposedly unflappable artist was upset was that he had been scooped. After this, Andy wouldn't be able to run an interview with Dracula. He'd been hoping Johnny would channel the Father's ghost, as others had channelled such *Inter/VIEW* subjects as the Assyrian wind demon Pazuzu and Houdini. Andy didn't prize Johnny just because he was a vampire; it was important that he was of the direct Dracula line.

He didn't feel the Father with him so much, though he knew he was always there. It was as if he had absorbed the great ghost almost completely, learning the lessons of the Count, carrying on his mission on Earth. The past was fog, now. His European life and death were faint, and he told varying stories because he remembered differently each time. But in the fog stood the red-eyed, black-caped figure of Dracula, reaching out to him, reaching out through him.

Sometimes, Johnny Pop thought he *was* Dracula. The Churchward woman had almost believed it, once. And

Andy would be so delighted if it were true. But Johnny wasn't *just* Dracula.

He was no longer unique. There were other vampires in the country, the city, at this party. They weren't the Olde Worlde seigneurs of the Transylvania Movement, at once arrogant and pitiful, but Americans, if not by birth then inclination. Their extravagant names had a copy-of-a-copy paleness, suggesting hissy impermanence: Sonja Blue, Satanico Pandemonium, Skeeter, Scumbalina. Metaphorical (or actual?) children-in-darkness of Andy Warhol, the first thing they did upon rising from the dead was – like an actor landing a first audition – change their names. Then, with golden drac running in their veins, they sold themselves to the dhamps, flooding to New York where the most suckheads were. In cash, they were richer than most castle-bound TM elders, but they coffined in camper vans or at the Y, and wore stinking rags.

Andy snapped out of his sulk. A vampire youth who called himself Nothing paid homage to him as the Master, offering him a criss-crossed arm. Andy stroked the kid's wounds, but held back from sampling the blood.

Johnny wondered if the hook he felt was jealousy.

Johnny and Andy lolled on the back seat of the limo with the sun-roof open, playing chicken with the dawn.

The chatter of the night's parties still ran around Johnny's head, as did the semi-ghosts he had swallowed with his victims' blood. He willed a calm cloud to descend upon the clamour of voices and stilled his brain. For once, the city was quiet.

He was bloated with multiple feedings – at every party, boys and girls offered their necks to him – and Andy seemed flushed enough to suggest he had accepted a few discreet nips somewhere along the course of the night. Johnny felt lassitude growing in him, and knew that after relieving himself and letting the Good Catholics go to work, he would need to hide in the refrigerated coffin unit that was his New York summer luxury for a full day.

The rectangle of sky above was starless pre-dawn blue-grey. Red tendrils were filtering through, reflected off the glass frontages of Madison Avenue. The almost-chill haze of four a.m. had been burned away in an instant, like an ancient elder, and it would be another murderously hot day, confining them both to their lairs for a full twelve hours.

They said nothing, needed to say nothing.

Valerie Solanas was the founder and sole member of the Society for Killing All Vampires, authoress of the self-published **SKAV Manifesto**. *In bite-sized quotes, the* **Manifesto** *is quite amusing – 'enlightened vampires who wish to demonstrate solidarity with the Movement may do so by killing themselves' – but it remains a wearisome read, not least because Valerie never quite sorted out what she meant by the term 'vampire'. Of course, as an academic, I understand entirely the impatience she must have felt with what she considered irrelevances like agenda-setting and precise definitions of abstruse language. In the end, Valerie was a paranoid sociopath, and the vampires were her enemies, all who were out to get her, to stand in her way. At first, she didn't even mean* **nosferatu** *when she referred to* *vampires, but a certain type of patriarchal oppressor. At the end, she meant everyone else in the world.*

*She is in one of the little-known films, **I, Vampire** (1967) – mingling briefly with Tom Baker as the vampire Lord Andrew Bennett, and Ultra Violet, the wonderfully named Bettina Coffin and a Nico-shaped patch of empty screen. She had various grudges against Andy Warhol – he had lost a playscript she sent him, he wouldn't publish her book, he didn't make her famous – but no more than any one of a dozen other Mole People. Billy Name has said that he was never sure whether he should kill himself or Andy, and kept putting off the decision. Oliver Stone's **Who Shot Andy Warhol?** is merely the culmination of thirty years of myth and fantasy. It bears repeating that the conspiracy theories Stone and others have espoused have little or no basis in fact, and Valerie Solanas acted entirely on her own, conspiring or colluding with no one. Stone's point, which is well-taken, is that in June 1968, **someone** had to shoot Andy Warhol; if Valerie hadn't stepped up to the firing line, any one of a dozen others could as easily have melted down the family silver for bullets. But it was Valerie.*

By 1968, the Factory had changed. It was at a new location and Warhol had new associates – Fred Hughes, Paul Morrissey, Bob Colacello – who tried to impose a more businesslike atmosphere. The Mole People were discouraged from hanging about, and poured out their bile on Andy's intermediaries, unable to accept that they had been banished on the passive dictate of Warhol himself. Valerie turned up while Andy was in a meeting with art critic Mario Amaya and on the phone with yet another supervamp Viva, and put two bullets into him, and one incidentally in Amaya. Fred Hughes, born

negotiator, apparently talked her out of killing him and she left
by the freight elevator.

It was a big story for fifteen minutes, but just as Andy was
declared clinically dead at Columbus Hospital news came in
from Chicago that Robert Kennedy had been assassinated. Every
newspaper in America remade their front pages, bumping the
artist to 'and in other news . . .'

Kennedy stayed dead. Andy didn't.

Conklin, *ibid*

The Halloween party at 54 was desperately lavish, and
Steve made him Guest of Honour, naming him the
Official Spectre at the Feast.

In a brief year, Johnny had become this town's favourite monster. Andy was Vampire Master of New York, but
Johnny Pop was Prince of Darkness, father and furtherer
of a generation of dhamps, scamps and vamps. There
were songs about him ('Fame, I'm Gonna Live Forever'),
he had been in a movie (at least his smudge had) with
Andy (Ulli Lommel's *Drac Queens*), he got more neck than
a giraffe, and there was a great deal of interest in him
from the Coast.

Cakes shaped like coffins and castles were wheeled
into 54, and the Man in the Moon sign was red-eyed
and fang-toothed in homage. Liberace and Elton John
played duelling pianos, while the monster-disguised
Village People – the Indian as the Wolf Man, the
Cowboy as the Creature From the Black Lagoon, the
Construction Worker as the Frankenstein Monster, the
Biker as Dracula, the Cop as the Thing From Another

World, the Soldier as the Hunchback of Notre Dame –
belted out a cover of Bobby 'Boris' Pickett's 'The Monster Mash'.

The day drac became a proscribed drug by act of
Congress, Johnny stopped manufacturing it personally
and impressed a series of down-on-their-luck *nosferatu* to
be undead factories. The prices of the product shot up
again, as did the expense of paying off the cops and the
mob, but his personal profits towered almost beyond his
mind's capacity to count. He knew the bubble would
burst soon, but was ready to diversify, to survive into
another era. It would be the eighties soon. That was
going to be a different time. The important thing was
going to be not drac or fame or party invites, but money.
Numbers would be his shield and his castle, his spells of
protection, invisibility and fascination.

He didn't dance so much, now. He had made his point.
But he was called onto the floor. Steve set up a chant of
'Johnny Pop, Johnny Pop' that went around the crowd.
Valerie Perrine and Steve Guttenberg gave him a push.
Nastassja Kinski and George Burns slapped his back.
Peter Bogdanovich and Dorothy Stratten kissed his
cheeks. He slipped his half-caped Versace jacket off and
tossed it away, cleared a space, and performed, not to
impress or awe others as before, but for himself, perhaps
for the last time. He had never had such a sense of his
own power. He no longer heard the Father's voice, for
he was the Father. All the ghosts of this city, of this
virgin continent, were his to command and consume.

Here ended the American Century. Here began, again, the Anni Draculae.

Huge, lovely eyes fixed him from the crowd. A nun in full penguin suit. Red, red heart-shaped lips and ice-white polished cheeks. Her pectoral cross, stark silver against a white collar, smote him with a force that made him stagger. She wasn't a real nun, of course, just as the Village People weren't real monsters. This was a party girl, dressed up in a costume, trying to probe the outer reaches of bad taste.

She touched his mind, and an electricity sparked.

He remembered her. The girl whose name was Death, whom he had bitten and left holding a scarf to a leaking neck-wound. He had taken from her but now, he realised, she had taken from him. She was not a vampire, but he had turned her, changed her, made her a huntress.

She daintily lifted her crucifix and held it up. Her face was a gorgeous blank.

Her belief gave the symbol power and he was smitten, driven back across the flashing dance floor, between stumbling dancers. Death glided after him like a ballet dancer, instinctively avoiding people, face red and green and purple and yellow with the changing light. At the dead centre of the dance floor, she held her cross up high above her head. It was reflected in the glitterball, a million shining cruciforms dancing over the crowds and the walls.

Johnny felt each reflected cross as a whiplash. He looked about for help.

All his friends were here. Andy was up there on a balcony, somewhere, looking down with pride. And Steve had planned this whole evening for him. This was where his rise had truly begun, where he had sold his first suck, made his first dollars. But he was not safe here. Death had consecrated Studio 54 against him.

Other vampires in the crowd writhed in pain. Johnny saw the shredded-lace punk princess who called herself Scumbalina holding her face, smoking crosses etched on her cheeks and chin. Even the dhampires were uncomfortable, haemorrhaging from noses and mouths, spattering the floor and everyone around with their tainted blood.

Death was here for him, not the others.

He barged through the throng, and made it to the street. Dawn was not far off. Death was at his heels.

A taxi was waiting for him.

Inside the hack, he told the driver to take him to the Bramford.

He saw the nun step out of 54 as the vehicle moved off. He searched inside himself for the Father, willing the panic he had felt to subside. His flight from the party would be remembered. It did not do to show such weakness.

Something was still wrong. What was it?

The nun had shaken him. Had the girl become a real nun? Was she despatched by some Vatican bureau, to put an end to him? The Church had always had its vampire killers. Or was she working with the Mafia? To evict him from the business he had created, so the established crime families could claim drac fortunes for their own. Perhaps she was a minion of one of his own kind, a catspaw of the Transylvania Movement. At the moment, Baron Meinster was petitioning the UN for support, and TM elders considered Johnny an upstart who was bringing vampirism into disrepute by sharing it so widely.

Throughout the centuries, Dracula had faced and bested enemies almost without number. To be a visionary was always to excite the enmity of inferiors. Johnny felt the Father in him, and sat back in the cab, planning.

He needed soldiers. Vampires. Dhampires. Get. An army, to protect him. Intelligence, to foresee new threats. He would start with Rudy and Elvira. It was time he gave them what they wanted, and turned them. Patrick Bateman, his young investment advisor, was another strong prospect. Men like Bateman, made vampires, would be perfect for the coming era. The Age of Money.

The taxi parked outside the Bramford. It was full night, and a thin frost of snow lay on the sidewalks, slushing in the gutters.

Johnny got out and paid off the taxi driver.

Familiar mad eyes. This was someone else he had encountered in the past year. Travis. The man had changed: the sides of his head were shaved and a Huron ridge stood up like a thicket on top of his skull.

The cabbie got out of the taxi.

Johnny could tear this warm fool apart if he tried anything. He could not be surprised.

Travis extended his arm, as if to shake hands. Johnny looked down at Travis's hand, and suddenly there was a pistol – shot out on a spring device – in it.

'Suck on this,' said Travis, jamming the gun into Johnny's stomach and pulling the trigger.

The first slug passed painlessly through him as if he were made of water. There was an icy shock, but no hurt, no damage. An old-fashioned lead bullet. Johnny laughed out loud. Travis pulled the trigger again.

This time, it was silver.

The bullet punched into his side, under his ribs, and burst through his back, tearing meat and liver. A hurricane of fire raged in the tunnel carved through him. The worst pain of his *nosferatu* life brought him to his knees, and he could *feel* the cold suddenly – his jacket was back at 54 – as the wet chill of the snow bit through his pants and at the palm of his outstretched hand.

Another silver bullet, through the head or the heart, and he would be finished.

The taxi driver stood over him. There were others, in a circle. A crowd of Fearless Vampire Killers. The silent nun. The black man with wooden knives. The black man with the crossbow. The cop who'd sworn to break the Transylvania Connection. An architect, on his own crusade to avenge a family bled dead by dhamps. The ageing beatnik from the psychedelic van, with his smelly tracking dog. A red-skinned turncoat devil boy with the tail and sawn-off horns. The exterminator with the skull on his chest and a flame-thrower in his hands.

This company of stone loners was brought together by a single mission, to put an end to Johnny Pop. He had known about them all, but never guessed they might connect with each other. This city was so complicated.

The cop, Doyle, took Johnny's head and made him look at the Bramford.

Elvira was dead on the front steps, stake jutting from her cleavage, strewn limbs like the arms of a swastika. Rudy scuttled out of the shadows, avoiding Johnny's eyes. He hopped from one foot to another, a heavy briefcase in his hands. The arrow man made a dismissive gesture, and Rudy darted off, hauling what cash he could take. The Vampire Killers hadn't even needed to bribe him with their own money.

There was a huge crump, a rush of hot air, and the top floor windows all exploded in a burst of flame. Glass and burning fragments rained all around. His lair, his lieutenants, his factory, a significant amount of money, his coffin of earth. All gone in a moment.

The Vampire Killers were grimly satisfied.

Johnny saw people filling the lobby, rushing out onto the streets.

Again, he would have an audience.

The Father was strong in him, his ghost swollen, stiffening his spine, deadening his pain. His fang-teeth were three inches long, distending his jaw. All his other teeth were razor-edged lumps. Fresh rows of piranha-like fangs sprouted from buds he had never before suspected. His nails were poison daggers. His shirt tore at the back as his shoulders swelled, loosing the beginnings of black wings. His shoes burst and rips ran up the sides of his pants.

He stood up, slowly. The hole in his side was healed over, scabbed with dragonscales. A wooden knife lanced at him, and he batted it out of the air. Flame washed against his legs, melting the snow on the sidewalk, burning away his ragged clothes, hurting him not a bit.

Even the resolute killers were given pause.

He fixed all their faces in his mind.

'Let's dance,' Johnny hissed.

Now Andy was really a vampire, we would all see finally, doubters and admirers, what he had meant all along.

*It has been a tenet of Western culture that a vampire cannot be an artist. For a hundred years, there has been fierce debate on the question. The general consensus on many careers is that many a poet or a painter was never the same man after death, that posthumous work was always derivative self-parody, never a true reaction to the wondrous new nightlife opened up by the turning. It is even suggested that this symptom is not a drawback of vampirism but proof of its superiority over life; vampires are too busy **being** to pass comment, too concerned with their interior voyages to bother issuing travel reports for the rest of the world to pore over.*

The tragedies are too well known to recap in detail. Poe reborn, struggling with verses that refuse to soar; Dali, growing

*ever richer by forging his own work (or paying others to);
Garbo, beautiful forever in the body but showing up on film as
a rotting corpse; Dylan, born-again and boring as hell; de
Lioncourt, embarrassing all **nosferatu** with his MOR goth
rocker act. But Andy was the Ultimate Vampire before turning.
Surely, for him, things would be different.*

Alas, no.

*Between his deaths, Andy worked continuously. Portraits of
queens and inverted Tijuana crucifixes. Numberless commissioned silkscreens of anyone rich enough to hire him, at
$25,000 a throw. Portraits of world-famous boxers (Mohammed
Ali, Apollo Creed) and football players (O. J. Simpson, Roy
Race) he had never heard of. Those embarrassingly flattering
likenesses, impossible to read as irony, of the Shah, Ferdinand
and Imelda, Countess Elisabeth Bathory, Victor Von Doom,
Ronnie and Nancy. And he went to a **lot** of parties, at the
White House or in the darkest dhampire clubs.*

There's nothing there.

*Believe me, I've looked. As an academic, I understand exactly
Andy's dilemma. I too was considered a vampire long before I
turned. My entire discipline is reputed to be nothing more than
a canny way of feeding off the dead, prolonging a useless
existence from one grant application to the next. And no one
has ever criticised elder vampires for their lack of **learning**. To
pass the centuries, one has to pick up dozens of languages and,
in all probability, read every book in your national library. We
may rarely have been artists, but we have always been patrons
of the arts.*

*Among ourselves, the search has always been on for a real
vampire artist, preferably a creature turned in infancy, before*

*any warm sensibility could be formed. I was tempted in my
reassessment of Andy's lifelong dance with Dracula to put
forward a thesis that he was such a discovery, that he turned
not in 1968 but say, 1938, and exposed himself by degrees to
sunlight, to let him age. That would explain the skin problems.
And no one has ever stepped forth to say that they turned Andy.
He went into hospital a living man and came out a vampire,
having been declared dead. Most commentators have suggested
he was transfused with vampire blood, deliberately or by
accident, but the hospital authorities strenuously insist this is
not so. Sadly, it won't wash. We have to admit it; Andy's best
work was done when he was alive; the rest is just the black
blood of the dead.*

   Conklin, *ibid*

Johnny lay broken on the sidewalk, a snow angel with
cloak-like wings of pooled, scarlet-satin blood. He was
shot through with silver and wood, and smoking from a
dousing in flame. He was a ghost, locked in useless, fast-
spoiling meat. The Father was loosed from him, standing
over his ruin, eyes dark with sorrow and shame, a pre-
dawn penumbra around his shoulders.

   The Vampire Killers were dead or wounded or gone.
They had not brought his true death easily. They were
like him in one way; they had learned the lesson of
Dracula, that only a family could take him down. He had
known there were hunters on his track; he should have
foreseen they would band together, and taken steps to
break them apart as the Father would have done, had
done with his own persecutors.

With the New York sunrise, he would crumble to nothing, to a scatter of drac on the snow.

Bodies moved nearby, on hands and knees, faces to the wet stone, tongues lapping. Dhampires. Johnny would have laughed. As he died, he was being sucked up, his ghost snorted by addicts.

The Father told him to reach out, to take a hold.

He could not. He was surrendering to the cold. He was leaving the Father, and letting himself be taken by Death. She was a huge-eyed fake nun.

The Father insisted.

It wasn't just Johnny dying. He was on the last link with the Father. When Johnny was gone, it would be the end of Dracula too.

Johnny's right hand twitched, fingers clacking like crab-claws. It had almost been cut through at the wrist, and even his rapid healing couldn't undo the damage.

The Father instructed.

Johnny reached out, fingers brushing a collar, sliding around a throat, thumbnail resting against a pumping jugular. He turned his head, and focused his unburst eye.

Rudy Pasko, the betrayer, the dhampire.

He would kill him and leave the world with an act of vengeance.

No, the Father told him.

Rudy's red eyes were balls of fear. He was swollen with Johnny's blood, overdosing on drac, face shifting as muscles under the skin writhed like snakes.

'Help me,' Johnny said, 'and I'll kill you.'

*

Rudy had boosted a car, and gathered Johnny together to pour him into the passenger seat. The dhampire was on a major drac trip, and saw the light at the end of his tunnel. If he were to be bitten by Johnny in his current state, he would die, would turn, would be a dhampire no longer. Like all the dhamps, his dearest wish was to be more, to be a full vampire. It wasn't as easy as some thought. They had to be bitten by the vampire whose blood they had ingested. Most street drac was cut so severely that the process was scrambled. Dhampires had died. But Rudy knew where the blood in him had come from. Johnny realised that his Judas had betrayed him not just for silver, but because Rudy thought that if he spilled enough of Johnny's blood, he could work the magic on his own. In the British idiom he had learned from Sid, Rudy was a wanker.

They arrived at Andy's town house just before dawn.

If Johnny could get inside, he could survive. It wasn't easy, even with Rudy's help. During the fight, he had shape-shifted too many times, sustained too many terrible wounds, even lost body parts. He had grown wings, and they'd been shredded by silver bullets, then ripped out by the roots. Important bones were gone from his back. One of his feet was lopped off and lost in the street. He hoped it was hopping after one of his enemies.

He has tasted some of them, the Vampire Killers. In Doyle's blood, he found a surprise: the drac-busting cop was a secret dhampire, and had dosed himself up to face Johnny. The knifeman, who had vampire blood in him from a strange birth, had stuffed himself with garlic, to make his blood repulsive.

The blood was something. He was fighting now.

Rudy hammered on Andy's door, shouting. Johny had last seen Andy at 54, at the party he had left. He should be home by now, or would be home soon. As dawn approached, Johnny felt himself smoking. It was a frosty all Hallows' morn, but the heat building up like a fever inside him was a monsoon-oppressive and threatened to explode in flames.

Johnny's continued life depended on Andy having made it home.

The door was opened. It was Andy himself, not yet out of his party clothes, dazzled by the pinking end of night. Johnny felt waves of horror pouring off the artist, and understood exactly how he must look.

'It's just red, Andy. You use a lot of red.'

Rudy helped him into Andy's hallway. The gloom was like a welcoming cool in midsummer. Johnny collapsed on the chaise longue and looked at Andy, begging.

Only one thing could cure him. Vampire blood.

His first choice would have been the Churchward woman, who was almost an elder. She had survived a century and was of a fresh bloodline. But Penny was gone, fleeing the city and leaving them all in the bloody lurch.

It would have to be Andy. He understood, and backed away, eyes wide.

Johnny realised he didn't even know what Andy's bloodline was. Who had made him?

Andy was horrified. He hated to be touched. He hated to give anything, much less himself.

Johnny had no choice. He reached out with what was left of his mind and took a hold of the willing Rudy. He made the dhamp, still hopped up on prime drac, grab Andy by the arms and force him across the lobby, bringing him to the chaise longue as an offering for his Master.

'I'm sorry, Andy,' said Johnny.

He didn't prolong the moment. Rudy exposed Andy's neck, stringy and chalky, and Johnny pounced like a cobra, sinking his teeth into the vein, opening his throat for the expected gush of life-giving, mind-blasting vampire blood. He didn't just need to take blood, he needed a whole ghost, to replace the tatters he had lost.

Johnny nearly choked.

He couldn't keep Andy's blood down. His stomach heaved, and gouts poured from his mouth and nose.

How had Andy done it? For all these years?

Rudy looked down on them both, wondering why Johnny was trying to laugh, why Andy was squealing and holding his neck, what the frig was going down in the big city?

Andy wasn't, had never been, a vampire.

He was still alive.

Johnny at last understood just how much Andy Warhol was his own invention.

Andy was dying now, and so was Johnny.

Andy's blood did Johnny some good. He could stand up. He could take hold of Rudy, lifting him off his feet. He could rip open Rudy's throat with his teeth and gulp down pints of the dhamp's drac-laced blood. He could toss Rudy's corpse across the lobby.

That taken care of, he cradled Andy, trying to get the dying man's attention. His eyes were still moving, barely. His neck-wound was a gouting hole, glistening with Johnny's vampire spittle. The light was going out.

Johnny stuck a thumbnail into his own wrist and poured his blood into Andy's mouth, giving back what he had taken. Andy's lips were as red as Rita Hayworth's. Johnny coaxed him and finally, after minutes, Andy swallowed, then relaxed and let go, taking his first and final drac trip.

In an instant, as it happens sometimes, Andy Warhol died and came back. It was too late, though. Valerie Solanas had hurt him very badly, and there were other problems. The turning would not take.

Johnny was too weak to do anything more.

Andy, Warhola the Vampyre at last, floated around his hallway, relishing the new sensations. Did he miss being a magnificent fake?

Then, the seizures took him and he began to crumble. Shafts of light from the glass around the door pierced him, and he melted away like the Wicked Witch of the West.

Andy Warhol was a vampire for only fifteen minutes.

Johnny would miss him. He had taken some of the

man's ghost, but it was a quiet spirit. It would never compete with the Father for mastery.

Johnny waited. In a far corner, something stirred.

He had written his own epitaph, of course. 'In the future, everyone will live forever, for fifteen minutes.'

Goodbye, Drella. At the end, he gave up Dracula and was left with only Cinderella, the girl of ashes.

The rest, his legacy, is up to us.

Conklin, *ibid*

Rudy could have been a powerful vampire. He rose, turned, full of *nosferatu* vigour, eager for his first feeding, brain a-buzz with plans of establishing a coven, a drac empire, a place in the night.

Johnny was waiting for him.

With the last of his strength, he took Rudy down and ripped him open in a dozen places, drinking his vampire blood. Finally, he ate the American boy's heart. Rudy hadn't thought it through. Johnny spat out his used-up ghost. Sad little man.

He exposed Rudy's twice-dead corpse to sunlight, and it powdered. The remains of two vampires would be found in Andy's house, the artist and the drac dealer. Johnny Pop would be officially dead. He had been just another stage in his constant turning.

It was time to quit this city. Hollywood beckoned. Andy would have liked that.

At nightfall, bones knit and face reforming, he left the house. He went to Grand Central Station. There was a cash stash in a locker there, enough to get him out of the city and set him up on the Coast.

The Father was proud of him. Now, he could acknowledge his bloodline in his name. He was no longer Ion Popescu, no longer Johnny Pop, he was Johnny Alucard.

And he had an empire to inherit.

The Vaccinator

'Not quite a parody of *Men in Black*, but a gently sarcastic reminder of how that film could have been if it hadn't gone for the blurry option. By the end of the story, otherness both disguises and signalises identity. As usual, we're the aliens. As usual in Michael Marshall Smith's fiction, it's just not convenient for us to acknowledge that. At the present time.'

M. JOHN HARRISON

'A wonderful plot . . . unique and often darkly comic style. Something truly special'   AMAZON.CO.UK

'Smith tells his story with marvellous wit and gusto'

THE TIMES

'The crucial thing about Michael Marshall Smith is that he is enormously readable. Once you have started one of his books, you won't want to stop. He has the talent to become an inspiration to a generation of writers.'   THE INDEPENDENT

'The best and brightest from Britain's genre writers. A lavish feast . . . a gourmet treat'   THE TIMES

'Fiction that is blessed by the devil himself'

DAILY EXPRESS

'A good example of what is best about the dark fantasy of century's end'   DREAMWATCH

MICHAEL
MARSHALL
SMITH

The Vaccinator

The right of Michael Marshall Smith to be identified as
the author of this work has been asserted by him
in accordance with the Copyright, Designs and
Patents Act 1988.

This edition published in Great Britain in 2000 by
Millennium
An imprint of Victor Gollancz
Orion House, 5 Upper St Martin's Lane,
London WC2H 9EA

THE VACCINATOR first published by Victor Gollancz in
2000 as part of FOURSIGHT, edited and with an introduction
by Peter Crowther

To receive information on the Millennium list, e-mail us at:
smy@orionbooks.co.uk

A CIP catalogue record for this book is
available from the British Library

ISBN 1 85798 760 8

Typeset by SetSystems Ltd, Saffron Walden, Essex
Printed in Great Britain by Clays Ltd, St Ives plc

Walk North up Duval Street in Key West, past the restaurants, fruit juice stands and T-shirt emporiums, and pretty soon you'll come to the Havana Docks. It's a tourist harbour, quite small, bordered on both sides by restaurant piers and not much used for seafaring beyond a couple of glass-bottom boats and a jetski concession. Mainly it's there for looking at, and eating by, and watching the sun set over. Also, stuff swims in it. Some days you'll see a manatee down in the water around the pier supports, and there's generally some Yellow Tail and Black Fin flicking around. You'd think fish would have the sense not to swim right up close to seafood restaurants, where people can look down at them and think 'I'll have one of *those*, please, with broccoli and a cold glass of wine' but evidently not. At night little sharks swarm in the underwater lights, so many and moving so fast that it makes you wonder if the whole sea is like that, right out to the invisible horizon, a twisting mass of creatures who barely know we're here and won't miss us when we're gone.

On this particular morning a man called Eddie was

sitting alone on the upper level of the East pier, feet up against the wooden railing and a cup of iced tea cradled in his lap. He was watching one of the tan jetski assholes going through his chops in the bay, showing the sparse tourists how much noisy fun they could have for a mere fifty bucks an hour. The skier hadn't fallen off yet, but there was still room for hope. Eddie was thinking that it would be best if it happened out in the bay, a long way from shore, and that if anybody asked he'd say he hadn't seen anything. It was early yet, barely ten o'clock, and the sun was just getting into its stride, glinting off the weathered wood of the pier, the swirls in the water below, and the fading edges of Eddie's hangover.

After a while, another, older, man climbed the steps up to the pier. He walked along the deck until he was level with where the Eddich was sitting, and then ground to a halt.

'Are you Eddie?' he asked eventually.

'I am,' Eddie said, without turning. He took another sip of tea. It was warm already, the ice long gone. 'And you would be George?'

The other man nodded jerkily, realised he couldn't be seen, and said that he was. Then carried on standing there.

Eddie levered himself upright in the chair, turned and looked him over. George was tall, late fifties, spreading around the stomach and thinning on top. Neatly pressed grey shorts, a blue short sleeve shirt with razor creases, dinky white socks – in general not the most hip person in the Keys that morning.

2

'Sit,' Eddie suggested. 'Standing there, you look like some kind of Illinois realtor on vacation.'

'Uh, I am.' George frowned, stepping back to perch on the edge of the nearest chair. 'That's what I am.'

'I know. That was a joke, to set you at ease. Didn't work, evidently. You want a cigarette?'

'No, thank you. I don't smoke.'

'Right,' Eddie nodded equably. 'You and everyone else. May you all live forever.'

George watched while the man lit up. Eddie was wearing jeans, cowboy boots, a loose jacket and an expensive-looking T-shirt that didn't proclaim him a member of the Conch Republic or have a picture of a very specific breed of dog on it or say that while he was only one year old, he had an 'attitude' – so it couldn't have been bought in Key West. He had short dark hair and a trim goatee beard, deep and sharp blue eyes. He looked late thirties, was lean but broad in the shoulders, and gave the impression that whatever he did, he did it fast and well.

'Okay,' Eddie said. 'All I know is what Connie told me. You sell land up North, and might have an unusual kind of problem.'

'Connie? That guy's name was Connie? Isn't that a girl's name?'

'Usually, yes. In this case it's short for "Conrad". You want to take the issue up with him then be my guest, but I wouldn't advise it.'

George nodded, looked down at his feet, quiet for a

3

moment. His mouth opened after a while, but then closed again, tight enough to make a popping sound.

For the time being, that appeared to be it. Eddie watched as some seabird – he'd never been able to figure the difference between the types, or why it would be worth knowing – dropped chaotically out of the sky and snatched something from out of the swell. George meanwhile remained silent.

'Here's what you're thinking,' Eddie prompted, quietly. 'You got involved in a conversation last night with a barman you never met before. You let something slip. A matter you can't even talk to your wife about, and now here you are, sitting with another guy you've never met, and you don't think you can tell him about it either even though you want to.'

'How did you know I was married?'

'Look in the mirror some time, George. I never seen a man look as married as you. Which is a good thing, incidentally.'

'I'm glad you think so.'

'Right. Approval's very important. Plus that's not exactly a small ring you've got on your finger.'

'So – am I going to tell you these things?'

'You are. Because you don't like hiding stuff. Like the fact you told your wife you were going out to bring back pastries or something this morning as an excuse to come here alone. But lying's becoming a habit, because you don't want to worry her, and that's making you do things like go out to bars when she's asleep in bed in your nice hotel room. And that's a dubious way

of life, George, because sometimes bad accidental things happen to guys in bars, and then it's going to look like you got some whole secret history you wouldn't even want.'

George smiled with half his mouth and one eyebrow. For a moment he looked like a man who closed a lot of prestige sales and was a local legend for giving junior realtors merry hell when they stepped out of line. 'Thanks for the advice. So why don't you tell me what my problem is?'

Eddie shrugged. 'You're afraid.'

'Of what?'

He obviously needed to hear someone else say it. Eddie said it. 'You think you're going to be kidnapped.'

George's face went complex, relief and confusion vying for the same advertising space. 'Kidnapped?' he said.

'What else would you call it?'

George suddenly looked very tired.

Eddie dropped his butt to the floor, ground it out with his heel. 'Why don't you tell me what's happening, and then I'll tell you what I think and if there's anything I can do about it.'

George started slowly, but gradually gained speed and confidence. He was a man used to conveying information, and his story was short and concise. Eddie occasionally asked for clarification, but mainly just let him talk. It took maybe ten minutes, and then George stopped and spread his hands, embarrassed, like a man expecting to be ridiculed.

'Okay,' Eddie said. 'In time-honoured fashion, I got

some bad news and some good news. The bad news is you are indeed shaping up to be kidnapped.'

All the breath in George's body came out in a rush. He looked like he had sunstroke. 'So what is the good news, exactly?' he croaked.

'I might be able to do something about it,' Eddie said. 'How long are you aiming to stay in Key West?'

George rubbed his hand across his forehead. 'Today's Thursday. We thought probably the weekend, leaving Monday lunchtime?'

Eddie considered. 'Should be enough. Relax for a day or two. Act like nothing's happening. You staying at the Marquesa?'

'How the hell do you know that?'

'Just a guess. It's a good hotel. I'd be staying there if I was you. You should make sure you're around late afternoon on Saturday. They sometimes have wine and cheese around the pool.'

George laughed shakily. 'I'll bear it in mind.'

'Go to Bug's Pantry on the way back: they have some nice stuff there, and it's different enough to the continental breakfast that it's not going to look weird you went out for it. Corner of Curry Street. They sell flowers too, and newspapers. One more thing. You realise this is going to cost?'

George the businessman came back. 'How much? And what kind of guarantee do I get?'

'A lot, and no kind at all. Take it or leave it.'

Eddie watched George think about the phone calls,

and the fax. About what had happened to his car. About his wife, and the things he hadn't told her.

'I'll take it,' George said.

'Need the boat tonight. A beer in the next twenty seconds.'

Connie reached for the fridge. 'He's for real?'

'I think so,' Eddie said. 'Those assholes. Jeez, my head hurts.'

It was four o'clock and Slappy Jack's was empty. It was a small bar, with lots of dark wood and battered stools and pictures of the old town in heavy frames on the walls. Was a time when Key West was the biggest town in the whole of the United States. Wasn't that way any more, not by a long, long chalk, and on afternoons like this you felt the town knew it and didn't much care either way. Big towns have to get out of bed in the mornings and go do stuff. Prove themselves. Key West just put its feet up and ate some more dressed crab and thought about having another beer.

Afternoon light slanted in through the window of the bar, twirling motes of dust and casting highlights around the room like someone was setting it up for a photograph and wanted everything just right. At this time of day, there were worse places to drink. At night it was a different proposition, packed with tourists too shit-faced or stupid to realise the name was a take-off of Papa's favourite watering hole, and not the real thing. Come to that, even the real thing wasn't the real thing any more. The real

Sloppy Joe's was too small and nondescript for modern tastes, didn't look enough like the real thing should – and had been superseded by a vast hell-hole on Duval which you'd have to be out of your mind to drink in.

Connie worked both the afternoon graveyard shift and the small hours, mixing strong cocktails and stuffing green olives with almonds. Big as Connie was – and he'd been hired as a deterrent to weekend warriors with Margarita hard-ons, and had spent a long time doing successfully violent things in New Orleans – Eddie was tougher. They both knew it, so that was okay.

'You want me along?'

Eddie shook his head. 'Not tonight.'

'Need anything else?'

'Just the boat.'

Connie went off to make the call. Eddie sat at the bar, sipping his beer. Not for the first time he wondered what drew them to Key West, the people who needed him. Maybe nothing, and five in three months was a coincidence. Perhaps without knowing it they found themselves heading in the direction of the Triangle. Or it was just Eddie's long-overdue good fortune, turning up in a curious package. Whatever. They were a lot easier to deal with than his previous kind of client, the type who insisted on working in Central America and driving around in expensive company cars, or who lived in the US but were just too dumb to realise they'd accumulated enough money to make them an obvious target. Doesn't matter how you've made your pile, a fat bank account is likely to breed a confidence which is a short step away

from being an asshole. His new clients were less rich and usually frightened half to death, and thus prone to do what he told them.

The problem was dealing with the kidnappers.

In the old days, when Eddie took a job, he always used to hope it was Colombians he'd be dealing with. There was a set way of doing things. You thrashed out the deal in a bar somewhere, over a few lines of coke. You negotiated for the bad guys to be paid a percentage of what they might have expected to get out of the kidnapping: in return, they didn't actually go through with it. Like a vaccine. Preventative maintenance. They got some money without all the grief, and the client got to stay at home with his family, not pose for those pictures with newspapers in your hands which are never flattering, and avoided being starved, tortured and probably killed in the end. Much more convenient for everyone concerned.

The Colombians knew the score, were professionals. You arranged the vaccine, it was a deal and it was respected. These days Eddie thought he'd settle for a bunch of whacked-out Miami gangbangers, rather than the people he actually had to deal with. They were nutcases, pure and simple.

The story George Becker had told him was similar to all the others he'd heard. At first it was an occasional feeling of being watched, and half-memories of dreams which frightened him. Then one night George had been driving home after working late and it had got a little weirder.

He and his wife lived out of town, in a nice house which had a wet bar and a media room and was far too

big now both kids were out in the world making the same old mistakes and calling them their own. Half a mile away from home George had been chugging along, listening to the local radio station, when suddenly it faded out. He wasn't too bothered, it was a lousy station anyway, but then the car's lights went off and he stalled. He slammed his foot on the brake but it didn't seem to make any difference: the car just cruised to a halt and then sat there, ticking as it cooled.

Nothing happened for a couple of minutes, other than the sound of insects and wind in the trees.

Then the lights flicked back on, and the radio station faded back, as if he were driving into its signal. George tried the ignition, and the car started immediately. He drove slowly home. He told Jennifer what had happened, and she shrugged, told him to take the car down to the shop in the morning. As you would – if you didn't know about the dreams, and she didn't.

He took the car down the shop. They found something to charge him for, but it was the usual bullshit. The car was fine.

Nothing else happened for a while. Nothing to do with the car, at least. Occasionally things in his workshop seemed to have moved, but you could put that down to absentmindedness. And sometimes the phone rang at odd hours, and when George picked it up there was usually nobody there. Once he thought he heard his mother talking, but the line was very bad and she'd been dead nearly ten years, so he wasn't sure.

He put up with this for six months, and had almost got

used to it, when it suddenly started to invade his work. George's office had two names above the door, and his was one of them. He and Dave Marks had built the business from nothing, and were now both immovable fixtures in the annual list of the top five realty producers in the state. He believed the building their business was conducted in to be as inviolable as their status: unbreachable, the castle that Englishmen's houses were supposed to be. George rarely called Jennifer from work, unless it was urgent, and she had visited him there only a handful of times. That wasn't what the office was for.

Then one afternoon the phone on his desk rang, and when he picked it up there was no one there – but the silence had a strange undertone that made it sound as if someone was, but they weren't saying anything. He tried to find out from the operator who'd been calling, but as usual they didn't have a number recorded.

A week later a fax arrived on the private machine in his office. There was just one line typed on it, a description of a place in a forest which at first meant nothing to him. The paper was otherwise entirely blank, without even the sender information at the very top which just about every fax machine in the world automatically provides. George threw it away, and that lunchtime found a bar a few streets away and drank vodka so no one would be able to smell it.

He was feeling hunted now, by something that wasn't even there. Thirty, forty years ago, long before he'd met his wife, he'd been unfaithful to a previous girlfriend – with a friend of hers. He was mid-twenties, he got drunk,

it happened. It didn't mean anything except for how bad it made him feel. He didn't call the girl, and heard nothing from her for over eight months. He assumed she'd done the same as he had – realised it was a silliness with no future in it, and tried to forget it had happened. But he didn't know this. Not for sure. There was still the possibility that at some point, with no warning, a disaster could explode into his life. Then one night he and his girlfriend were in a bar, and they ran into this other girl. She smiled on seeing them, and he knew it was all going to be all right, and he was so relieved he spent the whole evening babbling until both girls told him to shut up.

It was like that, but a lot worse.

He started fixating on the idea of their Florida vacation, only a few weeks away. He told himself that if he could just get through until then, it would be okay. Although he'd already begun to entertain some pretty odd notions of what might be happening to him, he somehow thought he'd be safe away from home.

There were two more calls before they left – one at the office, one at home. Jen glanced at him for a moment after he told her that the second had been a wrong number – again – and then went back to finding out what dungeon of homemaker psychosis Martha Stewart was plumbing this month. Something told him that, while Jen was without doubt completely unconscious of thinking this way, he wasn't going to be allowed many more wrong numbers.

On his last night at work, the car cut out again on the journey home. At exactly the same spot, in exactly the

same way. George, a cautious man, had taken the car to the shop only two days before, making sure it was in good shape for the trip down. They'd tried hard to rip him off, but only been able to find a few bucks' worth of tinkering to do. The car was fine.

The next morning they locked up the house, briefed the neighbours a final time about cat-feeding, and set off. As they pulled down the drive, George felt his heart lighten. They only did a couple hours' driving that day, to break themselves in gently, and stopped at a shiny new Holiday Inn in some little town whose name they didn't even register. The guy behind the desk recommended a restaurant a short stroll down the street, and they had a great dinner, much to their surprise – pleased to be roughing it and coming out on top.

By the time they got back to their room they were feeling the way long-term couples sometimes do when they're out of their usual environment and have had a few glasses of wine. Jen said she wanted to shower quickly, and kissed him on the lips before she went. George sat on the bed, listened to the water falling on his wife's body, and smiled a little at the pair of them. Old guys going wild in the country.

Then the phone rang, and it wasn't anyone he knew. Or anyone at all, in fact. Just the rustle of wind high up in the trees. The sound of somebody not talking.

He told Jen it had been reception telling them about check-out times, and did his best to pick up where they'd left off. He did a good job considering, but it wasn't the same.

There were no more phone calls over the next few days, as they slowly made their way to Florida, down the Gulf side of the panhandle, and then into the Keys. But increasingly George found his mind was elsewhere. The sentence about the forest, which at first he'd just dismissed, kept coming back into his mind.

He couldn't remember the place it described. Nobody would have been able to. It was both too specific and too vague – as if it were not so much a real location, as a type. It just said 'Three pines almost in line, with rocks all around and a dark mountain behind'. It could have been anywhere. The more he worried over it, however, the more it began to be associated in his mind with flashes of white light, with a sensation of breathless running, and with the idea that something may have happened a long time ago which he had simply blanked out.

In the hotel in Key Largo he woke up just after midnight. He didn't know why. There'd been no dream, no sound, nothing. He was just suddenly awake. He eased himself out of bed, swapped his pjs for shorts and a shirt, and slipped out of the hotel room. The sky was wide and very dark blue. There was nothing in it. He heard the sound of faint laughter, at a distance, and saw that a few people were still lolling around the Tiki bar by the pool. On impulse he walked over, and charged a couple of Manhattans to the room. When he returned, half an hour later, he got back to sleep without any problem.

The next day they arrived in Key West, and late in the

evening George had found himself in another bar, again alone, and talking to a man called Connie.

That was his story. But Eddie knew that George was right to think he hadn't heard the end of it. The nutcases had gone easy on laying in false memory, which was good and unusually restrained, but everything else suggested they were settling for the long haul.

Connie came back. The boat would be set up, with fuel and ammunition on board. Eddie stayed a while longer, drinking beer and helping stuff olives. A couple of tourists poked their head in the door, but Connie scowled at them and they went away.

It was a still night. The water was flat and calm. Just after ten o'clock, Eddie cut the engine and let her drift a while. It was extremely dark, the only light coming from the boat's lamps and the stars in the deep nothing above. He was five miles out, over part of the long reef which starts north of Miami and follows the coast down into open sea. During the day you could join a cruise out of Havana Docks, come and look down at the fish and sharks swimming around over the coral. After the sun went down the only people who came out this far were marine biologists who wanted to check out the nightlife on the reef. Tonight there weren't any around, which was good.

Eddie set the radio to send, lit a cigarette, and settled down to wait. The signal was a sequence of fifty tones, repeated in an order so complex it looked random. Wouldn't mean anything except to the people it was

supposed to. Meanwhile he checked his gun, which had seen service in half of Central America, two European countries and the backstreets of more than a few US cities. So far he hadn't even had to pull it on one of these jobs. But you never knew. He cleaned it, loaded it with shells, and then laid it on the table in front of him. He felt keyed up, but not nervous. Eddie had done many unusual things in his life. This was merely the latest.

Fifteen minutes later the lamp on the front of the boat flickered and then went out. Gradually the other lights started to dim, and then the boat was in darkness. Eddie picked up the gun, put it in his shoulder holster. It had occurred to him, on the first trip, in fact, that there was no guarantee it would even work. They probably had ways of affecting things like that, like the stuff they could do with electric power. But he felt better having it around.

The water around the boat started to become glassy, losing motion until it felt like solid land. Everything went quiet.

Then bang – the light went on. Eddie flinched, cursed, and refused to look up into it. The light came down like a cylinder, a circular beam that was a couple of times wider than the boat was long. Though it looked just like someone had turned the world's biggest halogen flashlamp on him, Eddie knew it was more complicated than that. The boat was now rock steady, and the sea within the beam frozen in place. The light wasn't just a source of illumination. It grabbed hold of things, and could pull them up.

16

'It's Edward Kruger,' he said, loudly, shielding his eyes with his hands. 'Turn that fucking thing off.'

There was a long pause, during which the light stayed exactly as bright as it had been. Then it dimmed – very, very slightly.

'I want to go to the island,' he said. 'I've got business there. And I want to go the old-fashioned way, because this isn't my boat. Okay?'

Another pause, and then the beam went out.

Eddie looked up, but as usual there was nothing to see. The boat lights slowly came back on, in the order they'd gone off. Eddie started the engines.

It took another twenty minutes before he could see the island. There was a single light at the dock, and he headed for it. The tying point was at the end of a long wooden walkway, as they often were on the Keys, because the water around the islands was so shallow.

In the old days there used to be an island on the chain called No-Name Key, a few miles north of Key West: presumably so-called because the early settlers had run dry of the creative energy required to name the hundreds of local bumps in the sea, some little bigger than sandbars with a couple of trees. That island was called something else now, he couldn't remember what. Something dull, or quaint, or both.

The island he was about to land at wasn't even called something as unimaginative as No-Name. It wasn't known as anything at all, and never had been, because as far Eddie could tell, he and Connie were the only two humans who'd ever been aware of its existence – and

17

Connie had never actually set foot on it. It wasn't on any
of the maps, and Eddie had never been able to find a
reference to it in any of the painfully exhaustive quasi-
literate local history books. He'd come to believe that for
most of the time it simply wasn't there. Some kind of
cloaking device, he guessed – in place for a very long time.

He got the boat tied up to the dock, and climbed out.
Took a deep breath, looking back the way he'd come.
You couldn't see the lights of Key West from here, or
any of the other islands. It was very quiet, just the sound
of his footsteps and a faint creak from the walkway
swaying in gentle time with the water. You might just as
well be on a different planet.

At the land end of the walkway was another light,
which showed the path ahead through the forest. Apart
from the dim lamps every couple of yards along it, the
path was the only sign of artificiality on the island. As far
was Eddie could tell, the rest of it was entirely covered in
trees and brush. He lit another cigarette before he set off.
He didn't really need it, but it was nice to have something
man-made in your hand. It was grounding. Rah-rah for
the humans, something like that.

After a few minutes on the path, he heard a sound
over on the right, amongst the trees. He stopped, listened.
Nothing. There weren't even any insects on the island
and it was deadly quiet. It was much warmer than it had
been on the boat, and humid.

He started walking again, and this time heard the
sound from the left side, maybe five yards into the trees.
He kept on walking.

And then he suddenly turned around.

Behind him on the path, caught and frozen, were three small humanoid figures. About four feet high and thin, grey in colour, with bulbous heads and large black eyes that looked like those sunglasses people were wearing a couple of years back.

He laughed. 'What's the matter, someone leave the cat flap open? Going to be trouble when they hear you're out.'

The little guys looked at each other, then back at him. One of them cleared its throat.

'Hi, Eddie,' it said. It voice was a poor approximation of human speech, more of a clicking rasp. 'You got anything for us?'

Eddie reached in his pocket, pulled out a spare pack of cigarettes. He tossed it to the nearest grey.

'Thanks, Eddie,' they said, in unison.

'Yeah,' he replied. 'Now scoot.'

They scuttled off into the undergrowth. Eddie shook his head. If they were his, he'd electrify the compound.

The path wound across the island for nearly a mile. Towards the end the ground rose slightly, and then gave out into a circular clearing. This was about fifty yards across, and was completely clear of trees and bushes. It was covered in short, manicured grass, soft like you got in Europe instead of the sharp and tough Florida scrub. In the middle were four armchairs – three of which were black leather recliners, the other the kind of worn affair you'd find in a cheap motel – and a standard lamp, which shed a warm glow for a couple of yards around. Eddie

19

walked straight over and sat in the chair that didn't recline.

'I'm here,' he said.

They kept him waiting for a while, as usual.

George, meanwhile, was walking back to his room from the Marquesa's reception, after making a dinner reservation for the following evening. He was one of those people who really enjoy their food, and look forward to it, and take enjoyment in planning where the next meal is going to come from. That evening – after careful consideration – they'd gone to Crabby Dick's on Duval, and had good steak and blackened dolphin while sitting on the upperdeck and watching people wandering past below. The Marquesa's bistro was supposed to be pretty good, so that was where they were going to be eating tomorrow night. George didn't quite have his whole menu planned out, but he'd made some ballpark wine list plans and narrowed his appetiser options down to two. Though at the last minute he might go wild and switch to something else. You never knew.

Planning food events was also useful because it gave George something simple and practical to think about. Jen had accepted his story about getting sidetracked on the way to buy Danish, and been touched by the flowers. They'd had a nice day, just wandering around. Stood on the Southernmost point, looked at Hemingway's house and all the cats, drunk their own volume in iced fruit drinks. Then spent a late afternoon hour around the Marquesa's pools: there were two, both small, hidden in

the leafy courtyards created when three wooden Victorian houses had been loosely combined to form the hotel. Jen floated around, gently paddling this way and that, while George sat in a chair wearing a T-shirt and holding a copy of the local newspaper. Though it was no longer an exactly recent development, he'd never quite got over the disappointment of finding that he'd somehow become housed in an older man's body, and preferred not to inflict the sight of it upon the world.

He watched his wife swim, glad that he'd gone to see Eddie that morning. He'd been nervous, and expecting many things: blank incomprehension, ridicule, or one of several different methods of extracting money. Instead he seemed to have been taken seriously, which for an hour or so had made him feel light-headed with relief. There was no way of telling whether the guy could actually do anything – could be that it was just a more complex scam than he'd been expecting. But he felt better for having done it, whatever happened. When your wife's touched because you bring her flowers and the only reason you did it is to cover up the fact you've been lying to her, that's a bad feeling. You realise that you should bring them more often, and that you'd like to, but somehow you don't. It mainly just doesn't occur to you. Unless you're hiding something, and the guilt that engenders makes you realise how much you love the person you're lying to. He didn't want to be covering up any more. He wondered briefly what percentage of flowers in the world were bought for the right reasons – then shitcanned that stream of thought and tried to read

a story about a local group of poets. He couldn't. It wasn't interesting. If there was a local poet in the whole world who wasn't shit then George believed he must be in hiding somewhere, along with all the good local artists.

That, at least, was what anyone peeking would have found in George's mind that afternoon. He'd grown very used to covering up what was actually going on in his head, because he was finding it increasingly inexplicable and disturbing.

At night the pool area was deserted, with that strange, restful atmosphere public places get when the public isn't there to clutter them up. It was dark except for a couple of low yellow lamps, the vivid blue-green glow of the pool, and a few stars visible through the palm cover above. George was passing almost exactly the same spot where he'd been sitting in the afternoon when he thought he heard something. At first he assumed it was another guest out for a stroll, and got a smile ready. No one appeared. He stopped, looked around. Someone had put in a lot of effort growing plants in and above the courtyard, with big hibiscus and ground palms and all manner of other things Jen would know the names of. During the day you could see geckos, some of them pretty big, running all over the brickwork floor. Maybe that was what he'd heard. He began walking again, and started quietly to scale the low steps around the waterfall which was on the way to their suite.

He was still a way from home when he heard something that sounded like a door handle being turned, and then Jen's voice saying his name in the form of a

question. As if someone had opened the door to her suite, and she'd looked up to see no one there, and wondered if he was playing a game.

George started to run.

'Eddie, my man – how's it hanging? How are you, guy?'

Eddie looked down from the stars, to see that the three reclining chairs were now occupied. He'd given up hoping to see how they managed to do that – being not there one minute and then there the next – but it still irritated him.

'Hungry,' he said. 'And bored. You get a warning from when the assholes shine the big light in my eyes, you got video surveillance on the pier. You must know when I get to this chair. So how come it still takes you fifteen fucking minutes to get your asses out here?'

'Touchy,' said the first alien. Yag was his name. He, like the two others, had the recliner tipped back as far back as it would go, and was lounging with his arms and legs hanging off the sides. 'Think Eddie's a little out of sorts this evening, fellas.'

'It's just rude, is all,' Eddie said, and lit another cigarette.

'You know we don't like smoking,' another of the aliens said. He was about six foot eight, thin and spidery like the others. His skin was the usual pale golden colour, and glistened wetly. The way they looked, you'd expect them to smell pretty bad. Actually, they smelled of spearmint. His head was slightly elongated but otherwise not too different to ours. He was called Fud, and he was pretty drunk.

23

'You don't give a shit about smoking,' Eddie said, not putting it out. 'It doesn't even do anything to you guys. You're just being a pain in the ass, as usual.'

'We do too care,' Yag said, stifling a burp. 'Everybody cares. It's a zeitgeist thing.'

'You bring us anything?' the third alien slurred. Eddie didn't know his name. The spindly fucker had always been too wasted to pronounce it. Maybe that was how that Key got called No-Name too. Always too drunk to talk.

Eddie pulled the bottle of overproof rum out of his pocket and lobbed it to the alien. It landed on his stomach and he went 'Ooof.' Then pulled off the cap and took a long pull, before handing it on to Yag.

'I had some cigarettes too,' Eddie said, 'But seeing as you guys don't like that kind of thing, I gave them to the greys instead.'

'What?' Fud demanded. 'Where were they?'

Eddie laughed. 'On the path. What's up with you guys? Masters of the universe and you can't even keep your pets under control?'

Suddenly Eddie found himself with the three aliens staring at him, and for the moment they didn't look so drunk.

'When we want a human's advice on how to run our affairs,' the un-named one said, 'You'll be the first to know, Kruger. In the meantime, shut the fuck up.'

Eddie held the stare. 'Your call. But with those animals screwing around like assholes the whole time and flashing lights over people's houses, sooner or later it's all gonna go wide.'

'It's under control,' Fud said petulantly.

'Yeah right. Like that stupid autopsy video really made everybody think it was just a hoax. You guys watch television ever? It's the greys who're flavour of the decade, not you.'

'We don't give a shit what your stupid fucking species thinks,' No-name shouted, jumping to its feet and jabbing a long finger at him. 'I've wiped my ass on brighter life-forms than you, shit face.'

The sides of the alien's head were pulsing slightly, narrow slits opening in the temples. Eddie had seen this happen before, and suspected it was a prelude to something bad. Longing for a straightforward Colombian or two, he was glad of the gun in his jacket, even if it wouldn't work. At least he could hit one of them with it, if it came to it. He stood up.

'Gentlemen, gentlemen,' Yag said, mildly. 'Eddie, calm down. Come on. Have a drink.' He held the bottle out to him.

Eddie took it, made a couple of inches disappear, and then passed it on. Fud drank. His temples stopped bulging.

No-name glared at Eddie a final time, hiccuped, and took a drink. He sat down, then grinned. 'Give us a smoke, Eddie.'

Eddie passed him a cigarette, lit it for him, his heart-beat gradually returning to normal.

'That's better,' Yag said, and kicked the ground so his recliner span in a gentle circle, making a quiet 'wheee' noise as it went. 'So, what you want to talk to us about, Eddie? Let's do business.'

'Man called George Becker,' Eddie said, sitting down. 'Lives in Illinois. I'm authorised to buy an abduction vaccine on his behalf.'

'Excellent,' Yag said, rubbing his thin, long hands together. 'What will the market stand?'

'Looking at him, I'd say forty thousand.'

'Then that's the price. Plus five thousand dollars.'

Eddie sighed. 'Why the extra five?'

'Because we feel like it,' Fud said, and the three of them cackled. 'You got a problem with that, ape-boy?'

'No problem at all,' Eddie said, reflecting that had these guys been a crew of humans out of Miami he could have just whacked the bunch of them six months ago. 'Forty-five thousand dollars,' he continued patiently, 'in return for which you leave him the fuck alone, stop freaking him out with phone calls and screwing with his car and faxing him and putting stuff in his dreams and memory and this shit about some forest with rocks in it.'

'Sure thing,' Yag smirked.

'And, of course,' Eddie said, having been caught out this way before, 'you don't abduct him either.'

'When do we see the money?'

'This weekend. And leave the guy alone in the mean-time, yeah? He's on vacation. And get a mobile phone or something. I'm sick and tired of schlepping out here every time.'

'You want us to come find you instead?' Fud asked.

'No,' Eddie said.

'So we'll see you here in a couple of days.' The alien

waved a hand. Eddie was dismissed. He got up, walked away.

As he disappeared down the path No-name said, with obvious satisfaction, 'Going to have to kill him sooner or later.'

Fud and Yag raised an eyebrow each.

'Eddie's okay,' Yag said. 'Does what he's told, doesn't talk to anyone, doesn't ask the right questions.'

'What do you mean?'

'Well,' Yag smiled, 'he didn't even think to ask if it was us who were buzzing this George Becker character.'

'Isn't it?'

'Hell no,' Fud laughed. 'Never heard of the fucking guy.'

'How were the weirdos?'

'Weird,' Eddie said, accepting the beer Connie handed him. 'Tell you the truth, they're really beginning to get on my nerves.'

'Why don't you just clip them, have done with it?'

'Yeah, right,' Eddie grimaced, and glanced around the bar. 'Jesus – what the hell's got into these people tonight?'

The room was crammed with tourists, apparently at one in a desire to demonstrate how much noise the human head was capable of producing. Sweating groups of guys and girls, quite a few husband-and-wife outfits, everyone happily talking and shouting and even singing – with the exception of a peaceable and remarkably sun-burnt couple sitting at the end of the bar, who appeared to be methodically establishing how many Golden Mar-

garitas you could drink before your brain melted. Connie saw Eddie glance at them.

'From London, England,' he said. 'Just married.'

'And I would care . . . why?'

'Whatever,' Connie shrugged. 'Just filling you in.'

Eddie sat and quietly smoked a cigarette, working his way through a bowl of pistachios and piling the shells neatly where Connie could brush them in the trash with one negligent sweep of his hand. He'd told the weirdos forty thousand on the assumption he'd put his standard ten on top. Fifty felt about right. The arbitrary and fuck-ass irritating extra five they'd stipulated left him with the dilemma of deciding whether George would go for fifty-five, or if Eddie had to take half rate this time out. Wouldn't be the end of the world, what with his over-heads being not much more than zero, but no one likes getting stiffed on a deal. Eddie in particular didn't like it, but he was exploring the notion on the grounds that not charging the extra might store him up some brownie points somewhere. He didn't really believe in karma, but every now and then paid lip service to it or some other edited highlight of a belief system, on the grounds that you never knew – and that someone who'd put as many people under the ground as he had did well to hedge his cosmic bets.

Meanwhile Connie served the bar sitters, kept half an eye on the customers who looked likely to be first in line to cause trouble or be sick, and filled the orders that Fran brought in from the outlying regions. Fran was a cheerful and tough 23, had big hair even by Florida standards and

tattoos on her wrist, shoulder and small of her back which Connie wasn't strictly in favour of. Wasn't his business, but he hated to see lilies gilded and he was of a mind that tattooing a woman's body was like air-brushing a pair of leaping dolphins into the background of the Mona Lisa, just to perk it up a bit. Fran, though attractive, had a voice which could bend trees when she was riled and Connie elected as usual to shelve the observation. Instead he reminded the English honeymooners that it was only just after nine and the bar was open until three and thus they could afford to take it easy with regard to volume of alcohol consumption per unit time. They thanked him for his insight and consideration, and ordered another couple of Margaritas. Connie moved them up to pole position in his internal list of People Most Likely To Pass Out Before Midnight, but took comfort in the fact that at least they were likely to do it politely.

Then he noticed Eddie turn his head sharply towards the door, and glanced that way himself. Two seconds later, George, the guy from the night before, came running into the bar. His hair was awry and his face red and he was panting like his heart was considering its options and leaning towards a CVA. Eddie was on his feet before the door had stopped swinging, and flashed two fingers on the way across. Connie quickly turned and sloshed out a couple of tequilas, yelled at Janine to get her butt out the kitchen and hold the fort a minute, and took the drinks out the side door.

On the sidewalk outside, Eddie was standing in front of George. He had a hand on each of the guy's shoulders,

29

and was talking to him in a low, even tone. George's eyes were wide and he was still breathing badly, his hands down by his side and trembling. His weight was only vaguely distributed over his legs, and if Eddie hadn't been there George would have been flat on his face in a moment.

Eddie took one of the drinks and held it in front of George's mouth. 'Drink this,' he said. George shook his head as if trying to flick water off it, eyes staring at some point on Eddie's chest.

Eddie grabbed his hair, pulled the man's head back in one sudden snap and tipped the booze straight down his throat.

George spluttered like a man pulled up out of deep water and went into a coughing jag that sounded as if tissue were coming loose. Eddie meanwhile tossed the shot glass at Connie, who caught it in one hand and handed him the second with the other. But when George stopped blinking and rubbing his eyes, they were focused back on the things in front of him.

'Sorry for that,' Eddie said. 'But things really are going to be a lot simpler if you just do as I say. You need another drink?' George coughed once more, and hic-coughed, then shook his head.

Eddie nodded, satisfied, and knocked the drink back himself. 'I take it something's fucked up,' he said.

George's finger had stolen up to his lips, and he was rubbing them like there was something ingrained there which he couldn't stand. 'They've. Oh. She's gone.'

When he'd managed these words he suddenly looked

around, as if he couldn't understand what he was doing in this place talking to these people and was seized with a desire to go running away in some random direction.

Eddie reached out, grabbed his arm. 'Your wife?'

There were only two salient facts. Jennifer Becker had disappeared. George didn't know where she'd gone. In the time from him hearing her saying his name and him making it up the steps to their suite, someone had stolen her away.

'When was this?'

George looked at his watch. 'Forty, forty-five minutes ago.'

Eddie pursed his lips, looked away down the street. Two things immediately occurred to him. The second was that the woman had been taken round about the time he'd been sitting talking to the weirdos. In other words, the assholes had sat there and set a price, all the while knowing that some of their buddies were already on the way to abduct the target. As it was, they'd been too fucking incompetent – or drunk – to even get the right human, but that wasn't the issue. The issue was that they were jerking him around. No one had ever successfully jerked Eddie around before, no matter what planet they were from. Not for long, anyhow, and never for long enough to tell the tale.

George started slightly when Eddie swung his gaze back at him. For a moment there was something in the younger man's eyes, something that made it very clear that Eddie wouldn't be your first choice of guy to have a fight with, unless you were a SWAT team on the top of

your game. George didn't know it, which was probably just as well because it was the last kind of thing he needed at that time, but he was one of only two people who'd seen that look in Eddie's eyes and lived to see the next hour. The other person had been Eddie's father, a long time ago, and he'd since died of his own accord.

'Well, George,' Eddie said, his voice eerily calm, 'looks like we've got a situation. They sent some guys already, you weren't there, they got your wife.'

George pulled his hand away from his lip, visibly tried to pull himself together. 'Has this ever happened before?'

'No. The vaccine was negotiated. Even if it were just our bad luck that the fetchers were already on the way, they should have been recalled. Hopefully it's an error. If it's deliberate, then it's moving outside the usual rules of engagement.'

'So what do we do?'

'First thing, you go in the bar and call your room. Check she's not back there.'

'But why . . .'

'They could have realised the fuck-up, dumped her back and she's sitting there not knowing what the hell is going on. Go call.'

After George had shouldered his way into the mass of people in the bar and was out of sight, Connie looked at Eddie.

'What's going on?'

'I don't know. I don't think it's a screw-up. I think it's deliberate.'

'Could be the greys?'

'I guess, but I don't think so. They usually do their own thing and don't mess with stuff the big boys have set up. Plus they know better than to fuck with me. After that last time.'

'What you going to do? Head back out there?'

Eddie shook his head. 'Not tonight. If it's a screw-up, I want to give them time to put it right. If not, then I'm surely going to have to have a word with them.'

'Want a hand?'

'Could be. You ever whacked an extra-terrestrial before?'

'Not as far as I know. They really bleed green?'

'You got me. I never whacked one either.'

They mused on the subject for a minute, then Eddie started getting a sinking feeling. They went inside and checked the public phone where it stood a noisy yard from the gents' toilets. Five minutes later the whole building had been checked, and it was for sure.

George had disappeared.

Sunrise found Connie standing out on the deck at Havana docks, on the off-chance. Eddie meanwhile was sitting on the little balcony outside the Beckers' suite at the Marquesa. He knew nobody was inside, because he'd checked. He'd also tossed the room and the luggage. Sometimes things got left behind. He didn't know whether it was because the aliens were careless, or if it was out of a desire to leave behind some kind of annoyingly meaningless clue, but on occasion you found little globules of alloy, or scraps of stuff which looked like

tinfoil but wasn't, that would make a UFOlogist hyper-ventilate. He kept meaning to throw it out, but hadn't got around to it yet.

There was nothing in the suite, except what you'd expect two older people to take with them on a week's vacation.

At a quarter past seven on the dot he saw a guy in a white coat approaching, bearing a tray of breakfast and the morning paper. Eddie quickly dropped around the edge of the balcony, and waited until he'd heard a soft rap on the door and the footsteps walking away. Then he flipped back up and helped himself to coffee. Way things were shaping up, the Beckers weren't going to miss it and Eddie strongly believed it a shame to let good coffee go to waste. The toast, on the other hand, he let lie.

He'd had plenty of time in the small hours, and all his thinking was done. The odds were that George would be a very long way away by now, beyond reach of anything Eddie could do help him. What had to be done had little to do with his client, though obviously he'd keep an eye out for the guy and his wife. Today's dealings mainly had to do with showing some skinny-shank weirdos that you didn't fuck with the way things were done. A vaccine was a vaccine: if the Colombians could understand that, then assholes from the planet Zog could too.

When there was still no sign at a little after eight, Eddie left the hotel and went to meet Connie down at the docks and get some breakfast with meat in it.

Meanwhile, less than a mile away, George was sitting

at the end of a long concrete promontory right at the opposite end of Duval street. Either side of the first half was beach, with a little restaurant down the way, but the last half poked right into the ocean and was in fact the southernmost point in the whole of the USA. That wasn't why George was sitting there, however. He'd already done the experience with Jen the day before, as a tourist thing, and actually neither of them had felt themselves come alive with excitement. It was a five-minutes'-worth kind of attraction, though as pleasant a place to sit as any. Truth be told, he had no idea why he was there, or how it had come to happen. He was just sitting, his legs dangling over the end, watching the waves.

After a while a woman came up and stood behind him. 'Come,' she said. 'It's time.'

A few hours later Connie was sitting in back of the boat, running the engine and slowly working his way through the beers in the cooler. Eddie perched up front, smoking. The sun was bright out on the water, and the ocean ran flat out as far as the eye could see. It was hot, in the dry clear way you only get when you're moving fast over water. When they were still a way from the right area, Eddie swore. He grabbed the binoculars and glared through them at a dot on the horizon.

'What?' Connie asked, speaking loud against the noise of the engine.

'Spirit of Key fucking West.'

Connie looked at his watch. It was just before eleven. 'Kind of early for them, isn't it?'

A glass-botton boat, capable of carrying fifty-odd tourists out to go stare at underwater things and be told stuff
by earnest people in white shorts, the *Spirit of Key West*
usually took its first cruise out of the Havana docks at
around midday.

'It's coming season,' Eddie said. 'Guess Jack reckoned
he could squeeze in a load of early birds.'

'It's going to fuck things up, isn't it?'

'There's no way the weirdos will uncloak in front of a
bunch of assholes with cameras.'

'So what do we do?'

'Any idea how long they stay out over the reef?'

'Never been. Got no real interest in denizens of the
sea, unless there's cocktail sauce on the side. Plus, like, I
live here. But shit, how long can you look at some fish?
Fifteen, twenty minutes? And that's assuming you're
stoned.'

Eddie swore again. 'I guess we just wait.'

Connie cut the engines and they drifted for a while. It
was calm and very quiet, just the hollow slocking sound
of water lapping up against the sides of the boat, and a
few birds running the avian commuter routes up above.
The sea bed was maybe ten, twelve feet below, mainly
bone-coloured sand but some white rocks and patches of
weed. Eddie knew that, in a few places in the area, if
you were to dig a few feet below the surface you'd find
unrusting metal caskets, places where the visitors stored
things that included the buried remains of both their
own kind and humans. But he had no real interest in
finding them.

They gave the boat twenty-five minutes, and then Connie got on the radio to suggest to Jack that maybe his clients had seen enough fucking fish and would he like to get the hell back into harbour.

After about a couple minutes of trying Connie gave Eddie a look. Eddie nodded. 'Let's go see what's going on here.'

It took them ten minutes to get within shouting distance. Neither of them especially felt like shouting, so they went in a little closer. The boat, a sixty-foot Seabreezer IV, was stationary near the reef, though a hundred yards more to the west than you would have expected. The engine was off. The boat was drifting. Eddie tried again on the radio, and got no response. Then he tried shouting anyway, in case Jack had slipped out of the control room for a cigarette while his passengers were down on the lower deck inside. Nobody shouted back.

Meanwhile Connie brought the boat in closer. 'So now what?'

'Bring us up right to the back.' Eddie already had a gun in his hand, and one of the big knives slipped down into his boot.

Connie picked up the other gun. 'And if they suddenly kick in the engines?'

'There was anybody on the bridge, we'd have spoken to them by now.'

They got the boat up flat against the stern of the *Spirit of Key West*, and tied her on. Then they climbed aboard, Eddie first, Connie second: neither of them especially

scared and both reconciled to the idea of shooting someone if the need arose.

The boat was a standard of its type. Open at the back
so you could catch some rays on the way to and from
the reef, a covered place at the front for sitting and the
eating of potato chips. At the prow, an area where you
could stand and pretend you were that baby-face asshole
in *Titanic*. A bridge area, and, below decks, the lower
section where you leaned on rails and look down
through the bottom.

There were no people in any of these areas. There
were also no bags, paperback books, jackets or other
signs of things having been left behind.

After checking each of the levels, Eddie climbed back
up to the top and stood and looked for a while at the
desk where you bought soft drinks and cookies and stuff
if you really couldn't go an hour without taking on some
kind of sustenance.

Connie joined him after poking around in the bridge.
'This would be unusual, I feel?'

Eddie nodded thoughtfully. 'That about covers it.'

'So what's happened to all these people?' Connie
capped a beer which he'd luckily thought to bring on
board with him, took a long pull, and peered out through
the windows at the tinted ocean.

'Obvious answer is there's been a mass abduction.'

'Right. That was kind of what I was assuming.'

'But,' Eddie said, 'I'm not sure that's working for me
as an explanation.' He accepted the beer from Connie,
took a drink, and then thought some more. Then he

lifted the hatch on the food desk and went behind. Opened the cupboards and fridge.

Connie watched. 'I sense the Kruger intellect working overtime here.'

'Where's the stuff? Where the cans and the chips and those boring fucking cookies?'

'They are, I take it, absent.'

'This boat's not going to come out on a jaunt without them. You take a load of tourists out here in the sun and then tell them they can't buy a soda, you're going to have a mutiny. People are going to lose their minds with worry and just go berserk.'

Connie shrugged. 'Maybe Karen didn't make it in this morning, and Jack just took a chance on doing a trip without provisions.'

'Right. Or maybe the weirdos had the munchies, and took all the stuff with them. I don't like either version.' Eddie got out his mobile phone, flipped it open. No signal. 'Go try the radio.'

Connie went forward into the bridge again. Eddie walked out back and stood on the sun deck, leaning back against the rail and watching the waves. He'd been holding a question mark in his head overnight. He was wondering if all this might provide an answer to it. Difficult to tell at this stage, but he was beginning to think it might. Trouble was, it wasn't clear what the answer might be.

Connie came out, smiling. 'Just spent a few minutes talking to a guy who was ready to shit a brick.'

'Jack's back at the harbour?'

39
..

'You got it. With Karen, and those perky dudes in white shorts from the Marine Biology place. Not to mention a muttering horde of sunburners who bought tickets yesterday afternoon and are really keen to come stare at some fish and been looking forward to it all last night, and are currently two short steps away from litigation. He's had to stand a round of free iced teas already.'

Eddie rolled his shoulders, flicked the safety back on and holstered his gun. 'There is something unusually weird going on here,' he said, 'and it's pissing me off.'

'So now what? Sorry to keep asking you questions and stuff, but this is, like, your area. Me, I'm just a spear carrier and happy that way.'

'What did you tell Jack?'

'Said we'd found his boat, it looks fine. Maybe we'd bring it back at some stage.'

'He's not barking for it now? We don't want to be dealing with some other guys come out here to fetch it.'

'Think he's sort of given up on the day. Sounded like he had started to face the situation with the aid of alcohol-based beverages.'

Eddie nodded. 'Okay. That's cool.'

'We have a plan?'

'We surely do.'

'Hurrah.' Connie neatly stowed the empty bottle in the trash and rubbed his hands together, his grey eyes sparkling with dangerous good humour. 'And what is it?'

'We leave the boat here, and get on with business. We

go have a word with the weirdos, outline our displeasure at the situation in general, and if necessary kick some butt.'

'Eddie,' Connie said, 'that's a fine plan.'

Jennifer Becker sat as still as she could, covertly watching the two aliens. They hadn't spoken to her in a while. That was okay. She didn't want them to. In fact, she didn't think she could bear it if they did. She was only too aware that her life as it had been up until now, which she had by and large enjoyed, was over. A conversation with either of the beings who were standing a few yards from her could only rub this in further. She had also grown tired of trying to work out what they were saying. Occasional English words floated to the surface in their discussion, which otherwise sounded like the gurgling of a boisterous stream in early spring, trickle-fed out of melting snow and gathering volume and speed as it found its joyous way down a mountainside. At first she'd wondered whether this was because the aliens didn't have words in their language for what they were saying, like the French said they were going to have *un picnic* at *le weekend* while *camping*. Or whether it was more like Mrs Lal, the woman who worked at the Vietnamese grocery store in town and who'd been bilingual for so long that she seemed to forget which words belonged to which country – and who often turned to yell at her husband in a stream of gobbledygook which sounded remarkably similar to what the aliens were

saying. But it was kind of an academic question and Jennifer hadn't found that she cared enough to pursue it very far.

Instead she was thinking about a friend of hers, Sally Dickens. Sally was the wife of one of the junior realtors in Becker & Marks. She was a little older than her husband Bruce, and Jen was a little younger than George, and the two had been close, up until a year ago. Then, little by little, Sally had started to act a little weird. At first Jenny had speculated her friend was having an affair, though she couldn't really get the idea to stick because while Sally was a really nice person – and great, acerbic company at a cocktail party – she wasn't what you'd think of as a hedonistic pleasure-seeker. Pretty serious, in fact, on the whole. Not the kind for sweated afternoons in darkness behind curtains in cheap hotels out by the Interstate, or hands held under the table in unpopular bars. Actually Jennifer thought that of the two of them she was more that kind of person, though of course she never had tested this theory, and had never even wanted to.

Then one afternoon the two of them had been having lunch at the quite good Italian that was part of the new mall and she'd pressed Sally a little, partly out of concern but also just a tiny bit because her friend's new twitchiness and silences had begun to get on her nerves. When your best friends start wigging out on you, it cuts at the heart of your life. Sally was already a few glasses of Chardonnay down at that point, and, after a couple more, and over the rest of the bottle, she tried to tell

Jennifer a story. About something she claimed had happened one night when her husband was out of town, involving bright lights, strange noises, and a period of time out of time.

Jennifer hadn't believed her, and maybe hadn't hidden the fact too well. It all just sounded like something off a TV show, not very imaginatively adapted. The people she claimed had come to see her had been normal height or in fact a little taller, and not looked like those grey things you saw pictured everywhere. Apart from that it wasn't even a very interesting story, and Jen had smiled politely and sat there waiting for a gap long enough in which to ask for the check. Making it worse somehow was the fact that Sally had a bit of salad stuck between her teeth, which made her look vulnerable and sad. It wasn't the kind of thing you could point out, however, not while you were being told that kind of tale. Just something that could nag at your attention, and maybe make you pay an iota less mind than you should.

Over the next couple of months she saw Sally only once, at a party. She'd been drunk, and looked a little thin, but stood next to her husband listening to realtor stories and laughing at exactly the right moments. Her eyes had been flat, almost dry-looking, and when she saw Jen she smiled a small, tired smile that made Jen feel like a five-year-old, sensing for the first time that sometimes things happened to grown-ups which were too dismal and complex for children to understand. They barely spoke that evening, and when they did, Jen felt a little as if she was talking to someone who for reasons

best known to themselves had decided to impersonate her friend, and had got the look more or less right but whose heart wasn't really in the rest of the job.

A few weeks after that Sally had tried to kill herself. Tried really quite hard, and only just failed. Since then she had been resident in a private place about twenty-five miles out of town. 'Depressed', was the official verdict: just sort of depressed about stuff, in general. From what Jen could gather no mention ever been made of an otherworldly fantasy being a source for the situation. Bruce Dickens was bearing up reasonably well, probably partly because he and a female client who was trying to sell her gauche mansion over at the golf course had really quite a lot of meetings out of the office. There were no children, so that was that.

One afternoon Jennifer had driven out to the Hospital or Rest Home or Facility or Nut House or whatever it termed itself. She had got as far as parking in the lot, and sat in the car for half an hour. Then she'd driven home. She'd told herself that perhaps it wasn't a good idea for Sally to see her, that an unscheduled visit might interrupt whatever programme the place had her on. Though actually Jen knew that the programme would probably entirely consist of colour-coded pills and little measures of heavily laced liquids, administered at regular intervals by brisk girls with dusty smiles. And really she just hadn't known what she was going to say, or how she should be, when the reality of the situation was that her friend had lost her mind.

Or so she'd thought. As she sat now in the grove of

trees, very hot, extremely thirsty and being herself one step away from being driven insane by what was happening, Jennifer avoiding thinking about how she felt about her current situation by realising, finally, how guilty she felt about Sally. It wasn't even that she knew now that she might have been telling the truth. That shouldn't have mattered. Jen should have been a better friend to her anyway. And she wondered, pointlessly, whether she might have taken the whole thing just a little more seriously if there hadn't been that bit of salad caught between Sally's teeth, and how many of her judgement calls – and those of everyone else in the world – were made on such a trivial basis.

She wasn't surprised, only slightly relieved, when the aliens stopped talking and one of them turned and shot her in the head.

And the sad fact of the matter was that Sally Dickens hadn't been abducted. She really had just lost her mind.

'I'm hungry, is all I'm saying.'

Eddie shelved the idea of stripping his gun down. He'd already done it twice. No good could come of doing it again. No good had come of doing it the last time. He looked up at Connie. 'If you thought you were going to need to eat, you should have brought some food. That would have been the thinking man's approach.'

'Didn't think I was going to need it, mainly because I didn't think it was going to take this long. This is a protracted fucking afternoon we're having here, not to say one that's beginning to drag.'

'Really? Funny you feel like that, because I'm having a fucking ball.' He irritably started taking the gun apart again.

Connie shrugged. 'I feel like an ass sitting out here. Plus my head is getting sunburnt and that I can do without. Not to mention we're running out of beer.'

'You think things are bad now, wait until I run out of cigarettes. Then you're really going to see a downturn in the situation.'

Connie shook his head. 'This is no good, Eddie. You got to make a change in your working conditions. What kind of fucked-up deal is this, that you can't just go find the guys and whack them? Got to be the bottom line of any transaction of this nature. People fuck you around, they know they're going to get clipped. It's motivational management. Keeps them perky.'

'Connie, I run out of cigarettes, I'm going to whack *you*.'

'I'm just saying. That's all. This isn't dignified.'

It was just after five, Connie should have been at work hours before, and the sun was dipping low in the sky – but nothing was happening. Nothing had happened all afternoon, in fact. They'd sat in the right place for a while, then got so bored that they went back to the *Spirit of Key West*, tied the smaller boat on back, and taken the cruiser back to the harbour. Connie's intuition concerning Jack's coping mechanisms had proved to be correct. There was no danger he was taking the boat out again that day, unless he had some way of working it by remote control from the barstool he was already in

danger of falling off of. The tourists had lost interest and gone off to spend their refund money on T-shirts and driftwood sculptures. And food, probably, Connie mused, wishing he'd had the foresight to pick something up before they turned round and came back out again, instead of wasting the time ringing the bar to warn them he was going to be late. It wasn't that he was so damned hungry, more that the idea had got into his head and, in the absence of stimuli other than waves and sunlight and seabirds, was proving pretty hard to dislodge.

Plus, actually, when he thought about it, he *was* kind of hungry. Eddie didn't seem to care either way, which Connie felt was weird. A guy had to eat, and breakfast was many hours ago and had anyway been compact and taken on the run. Eddie, on the other hand, seemed capable of existing solely on cigarettes and scowling.

'You never had to do this by day before?'

'No.'

'We can't just forget about the big light thing, go straight to the island?'

'It's just not there during the day. I've looked. It might be there at night. We have to wait and see.'

'Well, next time you'll know to bring a sandwich.'

'There isn't going to be a next time. Or if there is, it'll be a bazooka in the lunchbox, believe me. Look, eat a piece of rope or something, would you? I'm thinking here.'

Connie shrugged again, and opened one of the few remaining beers.

Meanwhile Eddie looked out over the ocean. He was

indeed thinking, and what he was primarily thinking was that this would all be settled pretty soon. Once the light went, the weirdos would be sure to pick them up. They didn't like people hanging around here after dark, as a few hundred years of disappearances testified. The only reason why Eddie wasn't on that list of anomalies is that the time when they'd picked him up and dumped him on the island he'd got the measure of the spindly ones pretty quickly, and had the balls to suggest a commercial arrangement to them. He'd known ever since then that the position was a perilous one. Of the three, he hated Yag the least, but he didn't trust him in the slightest. He especially didn't trust No-name. He'd met men like No-name many times, and they always ended up fucking you around. It was in their nature, even when it wasn't in their interests.

Eddie cleared his mind, set up what he knew, and what he suspected, and left it like that. It didn't do to do be too locked in one mindset when going into situations like this. The resolutions of violent events were generally short. You got killed, or you avoided getting killed – generally by killing someone else. That was what it came down to, and neither outcome took very long or could be meaningfully prepared for ahead of time. Like a tennis player facing a serve from someone you'd never played before, the best you could do was watch the other guy's feet, be limber, and skilled enough to whack back whatever came over the net.

So instead he thought for a while about finding a new line of work, but nothing came. After a time Connie

opened the last beer and offered it to him. Eddie shook his head, but winked: and everything was relaxed in the boat once more.

That evening the restaurants and bars of Key West did good business. Nothing spectacular, because it wasn't yet full season, but everyone went home pretty happy – the proprietors to nice Victorian homes in the Old Town or Scholz-designed palaces on the North of the island, the waitress and barmen to dwindling stashes of dope and rooms in ramshackle houses. Places like Crabby Dick's and Mangoes and Febe's Grill got in two solid covers of holiday spenders, and the Hard Rock Café doled out a hundred burgers or so, as an adjunct to its primary business of making people's ears bleed. The chi-chi bistros tucked away down side-streets and in hotels raked in by far the best money – the human species having lost its bearings to such a degree that it thinks small portions on big plates are the Body of Christ, and that running when you don't need to is in some way life-affirming. Meanwhile Slappy Jack's and Sloppy Joe's and Jimmy Buffet's saw good Friday night crowds, and the usual pilgrimage was made by many down to the Havana Dock to watch the night come, despite the fact that before, during and after sunset a uniquely talentless young woman armed with a battery of cheap synths polluted the air with jerky covers of the songs of yesteryear, primarily the mid-1980s, and especially those with a maritime or vacation theme, however tangential; while another woman, who had once been beautiful but was

49

now merely frightening, served long fruit cocktails in plastic cups and glared at the leavers of tips she considered insufficiently generous.

People walked up and down Duval Street in the warmth of the early evening, peering in stores, assaying menus, enjoying the company of their companions but with part of their minds distantly worrying about the children, pets, lovers and gas ovens they'd left behind. From above, the island was a patchwork of light and dark, groves of trees with house lights twinkling, a network of lit streets, the distant thud of music. You couldn't avoid the fact that life existed there, however far back you pulled: like a corner behind the fridge which never quite gets cleaned and is host to a variety of small microbular things going about their business with the happy, unmindful concentration of children.

This, or something like it but in heavier clothes and with no Internet access, had gone on there for hundreds of years – and would go on for hundreds more. What took place a couple of miles out to sea that evening never made any difference to anybody and was, as Eddie expected, over fairly quickly.

The light came on eventually, but only for a moment and nowhere near as brightly as usual. The sea never froze. For Connie, who'd heard about the light from above but had never seen it, the experience was kind of interesting. For Eddie it merely confirmed what he'd already decided: something was notably fucked up.

They waited another few minutes to see whether

something else would happen, but it didn't. Eddie cut the signal tone on the radio, and told Connie to start the engine.

'Which direction?'

'Straight ahead. That's where the island is.'

Connie peered eloquently out at the open sea. 'It's your call.'

'Yes, and I've called. Do it.'

They went fast and fifteen minutes later Eddie told Connie to slow it down a little. Connie took it back to pootling speed and watched as Eddie stood and looked ahead. There was still nothing to see. Eddie closed his eyes, got his bearings. He'd always been a good judge of space, even in the dark and in jungles and terrains he didn't know that well. It was just one of those things.

'I'd say we're a couple of hundred yards short at this stage,' he said. 'Keep taking her ahead, but slow.'

Connie drove. Eddie loaded his pockets with shells. Up above them the moon shed a cool, confident light that for several more minutes failed to reveal anything out of the ordinary.

But then, they saw something.

About twenty yards ahead. Something small and pale grey, about three feet above the ocean.

'Shit on me,' Connie said. 'What the blue fuck is that?'

Eddie didn't reply, but just waited until they were closer, by which time the question could be answered just through using your eyes. Connie slowed the boat right down, and then a quiet *thok* noise told them they'd found the walkway.

'Eddie, thank God,' the grey croaked. 'Boy am I glad to see you.'

Eddie tied the boat up, while Connie just stared up at the alien. Then he clambered onto the walkway. Not an easy task, while the pier remained invisible, but achievable.

He looked down at the creature. 'What's going on?'

'Weird shit, Eddie,' the grey said. 'That's all I know.'

'Do the tall guys know something's afoot?'

'I don't think so. They're kind of wasted. They even forgot to feed us this morning.'

'How many have you seen? What do they look like?'

The grey shook his head. 'Couple of the guys say there's four or five. Me, I only saw two. And those looked kind of like you do.'

Eddie turned back to the boat. Connie was still standing there. 'Are you coming up here, or what?'

Connie swallowed. 'Up where, man?'

'Up on the pier.'

'The invisible pier, I take it? The one where you're chewing the rag with something out of the fucking X-Files?'

'That'd be the one.'

'You know what? I'm wondering whether this is something I'm truly going to be up to on an empty stomach.'

Eddie leant down without a word and proffered a hand. Connie grabbed it, and scrabbled with relative grace up onto the walkway. He dusted off his hands and looked down at the alien, who looked back up at him.

'Hi, Roswell dude,' Connie said eventually. 'I come in peace.'

'That wasn't us,' the grey snapped, 'and I'm tired of taking flack for it.'

'Let's get on with this,' Eddie said, and started walking. The grey skittered round to trot in front. Connie took the rear. It felt like a good place to be for the time being. They walked the length, towards a yellow light. This, Connie observed, was also hanging a few feet above the sea. The situation didn't seem to be bugging Eddie, however, so he guessed it was okay. A couple of yards before they reached it, he got a flicker in his eyes. For a moment it looked like there was something behind the light, a body of land. Then the impression disappeared, to be replaced by a couple of oval heads around the light. There was some excitable chattering in a language that was neither English or Spanish, the only ones Connie had any real acquaintance with.

'Okay guys,' the grey said to them, as they got to the end. He nodded in the direction of the three other greys, who'd appeared from behind the light. All of them either waved or nodded at Eddie. 'What you have to do is get land-side of my buddies here.'

Eddie walked past the little aliens. Connie followed. The moment his back foot was past them, a whole island flicked into view. And this time, it stayed there. Connie shook his head.

'How the hell'd you do that?'

'Our science is many centuries ahead of yours,' intoned

one of the greys. 'Do not adjust your television set.' The others giggled.

Eddie shushed them, and explained his plan.

Minutes later the greys quietly led Connie towards the path, and Eddie slipped alone into the trees. He waited until they were out of sight around the corner, and then cut a wide path around the island. Partly this was because it would probably turn out better if they didn't all approach the centre from the same direction. Partly it was to see if there was any evidence to bear out a hunch which had been slowly gaining hunchiness all afternoon.

In a grove close to the shore on the East side he found the body of someone he thought very likely to be Jennifer Becker, lying awkwardly on the ground. Eddie didn't bother to check for a pulse. She'd evidently been shot by a weapon of non-human provenance, which had punched a hole right through her head. A sad, crumpled end for someone who'd never really understood the situation she'd found herself in, but then Eddie could have said the same for many people he'd known, who'd fallen in the kind of fights that got covered on CNN, and then been buried with full military honours. All around her in the sand were two sets of footprints of pretty normal shape and size. One of them bore the logo of a prominent earthling casualware manufacturer. The other showed all the signs of having been made by flip flops of equally terrestrial provenance.

Eddie decided he finally knew what was going on.

*

'So who the hell are you?' Fud demanded, glaring at Connie.

Connie looked right back at the alien. He'd already endured having his monkey-derived ancestry cited, and was rapidly discovering the truth of something Eddie had once told him: it didn't take very long in the company of these people before you started really, really wanting to kill them.

'Friend of Eddie's,' he said. 'He sent me here.'

'Eddie's an asshole,' slurred the No-name alien. 'I always said so. You're probably an asshole too.' He coughed, and then added in a wheedling voice: 'Did he send any smokes with you?'

Yag, who'd yet to say anything, shushed his colleague with a thoughtful wave of his hand, and carried on looking at Connie.

No-name hiccoughed and stomped away to flop down into one of the reclining chairs. The greys meanwhile were standing together in a protective huddle a few feet away, under the standard lamp as if for warmth. Most of them were casting wary glances into the trees which stood all around the grassed clearing. The one who'd met them on the pier, who so far as Connie could tell was entirely indistinguishable from the others except that he was a little bit braver, coughed nervously.

'He told us to come warn you,' the little alien said to Yag. The others stopped peering around and gathered behind him, for moral support. 'Some bad stuff is happening. The guy he was arranging a vaccine for has disappeared. Plus his wife.'

'Wasn't us,' Fud said. 'We never heard of the guy.'

'He knows,' said the grey. 'Think he's going to want a word with you about that. And you know what he's like when he's pissed off.'

'So who was it?' Yag asked.

'Us,' said a voice, and three species whirled at once.

Standing at the edge of the clearing was a man. Tall, dressed in grey shorts and nothing else. He'd lost the rest of his clothes during the day, no longer able to remember why he had to wear them. Only a shadowy vestige of an old propriety had kept the shorts in position. He stood in shadow, and at first Connie couldn't see his face. Then he took a couple of shambling paces forward, legs twisting as if he'd been knee-capped but was still somehow able to support his weight, a gun pointed in the general direction of the spindly aliens. Yag and Fud took small steps backwards.

No-name peered at the human and belched quietly. 'What the crap,' he rasped, 'is happening now?'

The man turned from the waist, as if he'd forgotten about his legs, and pointed the gun directly at him. 'Shut up,' he said.

'How did you get here, George?' Connie asked, his voice remarkably level. 'What happened to you last night?'

'By boat,' George said, his voice inflectionless. 'It had glass in the bottom. There were no sodas though. Jen was with us. But then she died. Well, we killed her, in fact. It was very sad.'

'Hold on,' said Yag, frowning. 'What do you mean,

"us"? There's only one of you.' The alien was hungover to hell and back, and something was telling him this might be a bad time to be in that condition. Also that it would have been a good idea to have thought to bring some weapons out with them, even some teeny little ones, when the greys and human had appeared in the clearing.

If in doubt, bring a weapon. It seemed so obvious now.

'And,' Connie added, spotting another flaw, 'you're one of the people who's been kidnapped, surely.'

'He's referring to me,' said another voice, female this time. A young woman stepped out of the shadows on the other side of the clearing. She had big hair, dainty tattoos, and a gun in her hand that looked like a bunch of big spiders fighting on a frog. 'You got a gun, Connie?' she said. 'Sure you do. Take it out, slowly, and throw it on the ground.'

'Fran?' Connie asked, his voice finally cracking, 'What in Christ's name are you doing here?'

'Could ask the same of you. But I'm not going to, because to be frank I don't really care. Just lose the piece.'

Connie reached into his pocket like a man in a daze, pulled out the gun, and dropped it on the ground.

'Great,' muttered Fud. 'Thanks for your help, banana-boy.'

'Yeah?' Connie said, still staring at Fran. 'Well, you're so tough, you do something.'

'We're not good at that kind of thing,' Fud admitted.

Fran motioned George forward with her gun. George

picked Connie's weapon up and held it in his hand, as if unsure how to proceed. In the light that was always present in the clearing he appeared strange, shaky, as if holding himself together by will-power alone. His face looked bulbous and pale, his skin damp.

Connie shook his head. 'Is Janine running the bar by herself?' he asked, evidently in need of clinging to something he could understand. 'It's Friday night. She's going to go ape.'

'No pun intended, presumably,' Fran smiled. 'I have no idea. I don't give a shit. I hate that bar. And those olive things you do? What are they about? Are they supposed to be food, or what? They're crap. Now, to business.' She pointed her gun at his head. 'You know too much. You have to die.' She laughed delightedly. 'Cool. I always wanted to say that.'

'I know shit,' Connie said hurriedly. 'Really.'

Fran did something to the gun which was clearly preparatory to using it to hurt people. 'Sorry, but that's the way it's got to be.'

'Seriously, it's overkill. There's fish in the bay got more idea of what's going on than me. Far as I know, you're just a waitress. A damned fine one, don't get me wrong. But a waitress, mainly.'

'Oh, I'm a lot more than that,' Fran laughed. 'In fact, I'm . . .'

There was a sudden, short cry. Everyone turned, to see that George was now lying on his back on the ground with the air of someone who would be there for a while.

Standing beside him, his gun pointed unswervingly at Fran's head, was Eddie.

Connie didn't think he'd ever been so pleased to see in anyone in his life, and in that moment, in a tiny, very male way, he loved the guy to bits. Eddie looked so casual. He looked so armed. He looked so much like if Fran even twitched then she'd be missing her head before she knew it – which, though a very specific way to look, was easy to recognise and good to see.

No-name goggled. 'Are you seeing this too?' he hissed to Fud, in a low voice. 'People just keep appearing.'

'Yo, Fran,' Eddie said, carefully taking a couple of steps forward. His gun, while he did this, remained so steady that you could have rested a full beer glass on it and not lost a drop. 'If that's your real name. Which frankly I doubt. Why don't you lower the gun.'

'Fuck you,' Fran said.

There was a quick, dry cracking sound, and Fran's right hand disappeared, taking the gun with it. She blinked, and a moment later a thick black gloop began to drip from the severed wrist. 'You fucker,' she said, with quiet amazement.

'Why don't you tell Connie what you are?' Eddie suggested.

'He doesn't want to know,' Fran snarled, shaking her wrist. 'Jeez, Eddie, have you any idea how long it's going to take to grow a hand back? Fingers are really hard to do.'

'Fran's from another planet,' Eddie said to Connie,

slowly letting the gun drop. His tone suggested this was no more remarkable than her being a Pisces, or lifelong Blue Jays fan.

'I see,' Connie said, nodding sagely.

'So's George, though he didn't know it.'

Connie stopped nodding and stared at Eddie, like an owl which believed someone was trying to pull a fast one on it. 'Kind of hard thing to forget, wouldn't you say?'

'I'd have thought so, but that's what happened. For the whole of his life George believed he was just a regular guy who sold people houses and land. Jen believed that too, which must have made this afternoon rather difficult for her. But recently he's started to remember – because someone began dumping clues in his head. He thought it was a memory of abduction, and I assumed it was these assholes gearing up to make a play.' He indicated the spindly aliens, who were all wide-eyed and silent. 'And you guys didn't go out of your way to correct my mistake, which pisses me off somewhat. Given that I've now saved your gill-headed asses, I think there's going to be a change in pay and working conditions.'

'Saved our asses?' Yag said. 'How so?'

'This is some kind of significant staging post or trans-dimensional transportation thing you've got going on this island, right? And it's your job to guard it.'

'There's an element of that,' Yag admitted cagily. 'How do you know?'

'Worked it out. I figure that if there's a whole universe out there, chances are there's going to be more than one

type of alien and their pets around.' He nodded at the greys. 'No offence, fellas.'

'None taken,' the lead grey said. 'Hell, we like being pets. People give you food.'

'Sometimes,' one of the others added, pointedly.

Eddie turned back to Yag. 'Fran, she's not one of yours, so obviously she's one of a different type. Her attitude seems somewhat hostile. I didn't know from the beginning she was in on what's going on, but I figured someone other than George had to be – especially after George disappeared. My guess is that somehow, at some point in the past, she must have slipped through immigration and has been lying low. And last night I realised George wasn't what he seemed or even what he thought he was himself. When I asked him how long ago it was since his wife had been abducted, he told me forty-five minutes.'

'And?' Connie asked. He took a couple of steps away from Fran, who was glaring unhappily at Eddie. 'So what?'

'Takes about ten to get from the Marquesa to Slappy's,' Eddie said, 'Even if you were slow and got lost. Maybe he spent ten other minutes tearing his hair out in the hotel suite, or running around the grounds. Still leaves a block of time unaccounted for. I think he spent that time sitting staring into space in the room. I think that Fran abducted Jennifer as part of a process of getting George to remember what he really was.'

'What, like, gay or something?'

'No,' Eddie said patiently. 'George is a sleeper. An alien

in disguise even to himself. She needed him to wake up, because she wanted him to help her take this base and open the floodgates.'

'So why'd George admit it was forty-five minutes?' Yag said. 'Why didn't he lie?'

'He'd stopped being wholly human,' Eddie shrugged. 'But hadn't yet reverted to his real type. He was confused. He no longer really understood what to say, or how to say it. When we saw him at the bar, the human part was temporarily back in control again. He didn't understand what the hell was going on, and he was afraid, and he told the truth because he thought it would help. He'd lost his wife. He wanted her back.'

'Hang on,' Connie said. 'Fran was in the bar at the time. How'd she do the Mrs Becker thing, when she was carrying drinks in front of my eyes?'

'I don't know,' Eddie admitted irritably. 'I also never understood the appeal of Seinfield, and the whole grassy knoll thing is a mystery to me too. I haven't got the complete thing worked out. But that's basically how it happened, right, Fran?'

Fran had stopped shaking her hand. She looked calmly back at Eddie.

'Four hundred and fifty years,' she said, eventually. She didn't look defeated, or worried, or frightened. 'I volunteered. I came ahead. I knew Florida when it was just a big swamp, just a few Indians wandering around. It seemed like a good place to wait for backup. It was quiet. It was hot. Then the white guys showed up. Decided this was Heaven on Earth. Whacked the first lot

of Indians, and then let some more in and called them Seminoles. Let them stay. For a while, and then whacked them for the most part too. Meanwhile drained and farmed and did stuff, turning the mainland into a zoo. Then there was that stupid-ass fight about whether you were allowed to own other humans or not, so I came down the Keys to get out of the way. Watched the hotel guy, what was his name, Flagler? – lousy lay, whatever he was called – build the bridge right down through the Keys. Then the hurricane took it a couple years later. Then another got built.'

Eddie was keen on the idea of a cigarette by this point, but knew it would ruin Fran's sense of occasion and he figured that after a few centuries she had a right to that. Plus he was running very low. He just listened. The others did too. You sort of had to.

'All the time,' Fran said, shaking her head. 'You guys have no idea that you're all just barely tolerated guests, and that these guys,' – she indicated Yag and Fud with distaste – 'have already laid claim. I wait, and I wait. They said they were going to send more after me. That there'd be enough for us to take this ridiculous island, which small though it is, is very fucking important in the general scheme of things. That was my job. But no one appeared. No one. For year after year after year. Until finally I learned what had happened. I got a message.'

'How?' Eddie asked, intrigued.

'They're beamed in, coded into the Jerry Springer Show,' Fran said. 'What else do you think is the point of that shit? Anyhow, the message told me that the controls

had been tightened. They had managed to get someone over, but up in the North – and he'd only been able to stay for less than five hours. So he'd popped through, made a baby with a human, and then slipped back again. That baby was George, and he had no idea who he was. Until I finally found him, and started floating things into his head, waking him up to the way he should be. He got drawn down here, as all the sad abductee fucks do because they know something's going on around here and they think it's going to help them to be near. He still wasn't really getting with the programme until last night, when I got a wino to go around to the Marquesa and grab the little woman out of her suite. And that about brings us up to date.'

Everyone looked at her for a moment. Then Eddie spoke again. 'All that waiting, just for one more guy to arrive?'

'One is all I need,' Fran said. 'Hell, one good man is all anyone needs.'

'And now it's all screwed,' Connie said, with satisfaction.

Fran laughed, with a kind of quiet contentment. 'Screwed? I don't think so.' She nodded at where George was lying prone. 'I really don't think that at all.'

Eddie was quick. He turned, stepped back and put three shells into George before anyone else had even moved. But it made no difference. By the time the erstwhile realtor was on his feet, his body was already halfway to changing. His knees had swollen to twice their usual size, and the skin was splitting like a dropped

fig. The rest of his body was swelling too, unevenly but very quickly – some parts looking like their were about to explode, others dwindling to twig thickness.

'Oh, shit,' Yag said, in a quiet, aghast voice. 'It's one of *them*.'

Eddie popped a measured three shells directly into what had been George's head, but was now a huge twisted thing that look like an old tree trunk covered in moss. It made no difference. Then he heard the greys gasp, and turned to see the same thing was happening to Fran. She was getting bigger. She was expanding and contracting in the same way George was, but as part of the process both of them were simply acquiring more mass. Somehow, drawn from somewhere, more stuff was going into them – and they were getting larger and larger. Both were making a low keening sound, though it wasn't clear whether this was coming from what was left of their mouths or if it was part of the process of change, flesh and bone screaming as it was pulled agonisingly into a configuration never meant to spend time on this planet or in our reality. It looked like something that Hellraiser dude might have come up with, the morning after far too much Mexican food.

As the creatures got bigger and bigger, and started to vibrate like gross, blood-spitting tuning forks, everyone suddenly drew breath and realised they wanted to be somewhere else. Yag and Fud ran to a point on the left-hand side of the clearing and started hammering their fists on something Eddie couldn't see, but assumed was the means of going back whence they'd come. Evidently

it wasn't opening. The greys meanwhile ran in five random directions, got scared after a couple of yards, and then all hurtled back again to crash together in the middle. The two weirdos gave up on the invisible door and tried to go sprinting off into the trees, only to find that something had happened to the air there and it had become an invisible wall. No-name, meanwhile, was evidently trying to crawl underneath one of the reclining chairs. Connie just stood, hands down by his side, watching events unfold with the air of a man who'd decided that if the world was going to drive him stark raving mad he might as well go along for the ride, and get the full value out of the experience.

Within two long minutes Fran and George stood ten feet high, looking like twisted figures painted by Francis Bacon around an idea by Miro, rendered in blood and bloat. They took a few shambling steps towards each other. Then stopped, at what looked like a prescribed distance, and stretched out to each other with what had once been hands.

Eddie knew what was about to happen, and emptied his gun into various parts of their anatomies, without much hope but knowing that he had to prevent the two of them becoming one. Fran had said that's all she needed, just one other of her species. Eddie didn't want to see, didn't want the *world* to see, what happened when two of these guys conjoined. He sensed it would be a bad thing.

He shouted at Connie and Connie slowly drew his eyes

from the spectacle, realised what Eddie wanted, and pulled his gun.

They fired and reloaded, fired and reloaded, picking small divots out of the aliens' flesh but doing nothing to stop the inexorable progress of each's flesh towards the other's. The two bodies were now of slightly different shape, like halves of a biological jigsaw puzzle waiting to be fitted together like sperm and egg.

The greys and the weirdos stopped trying to run and just watched transfixed, as the two humans stood mere yards from the twisting nightmare and fired and fired and fired. In Eddie's mind everything in the world had disappeared. Everything within vision, everything he had seen and done and heard about, everyone he had known and killed and kissed and loved and found merely irritating. All he could see were two lumpen hands, straining towards each other, warm, glistening knobs of flesh yearning to become one thing and grow together. He hit the knobs time and again, but within seconds they were back again: while human fingers might be difficult to do, these creatures' real shape could evidently heal and regrow almost instantaneously. Eddie was coldly aware that such a species would be impossible to fight, once they came through, and that the fate of the whole planet might depend on him doing something now, that his mother's son held the future of the world in his hands.

He gave it his best shot. He tried. He couldn't do it.

And so it was just as well that, as the bridge was made and the two hands became one with a sound that was

like a hundred happy people sighing at once, there was the sudden noise of a vicious, fizzing explosion. At that very same moment the whole collective top half of both what had once been George and what had never been Fran disappeared like dirt scraped off a windshield.

The remaining four-foot-high pieces shuddered, squirmed like sentient piles of shit, and then were blown to dust by two further explosions of the same kind.

The clearing was utterly silent for a moment. Everyone stood and stared at where the action had been, seeing only a large circle of scorched grass.

Then they turned.

Standing off to one side, each holding a complex-looking weapon and still looking sunburnt, were a pair of English honeymooners.

'Sorry we're late,' they said.

About half an hour later Eddie and Connie stood at the end of the pier. The greys were gone. They'd been sent back to their compound and had complied with reasonably good grace, largely because of the promise of some extra food and being allowed to stay up late. The weirdos were also absent. The two young English people had taken them off to one side in the clearing and had a long conversation with them, during which there had been much kicking of heels, sulky nodding and general averting of gaze by the spindly ones.

Eddie and Connie stood right where they'd been, guns still in hand, waiting for everything to start making sense. Eventually the weirdos had come reluctantly over, obvi-

ously sent by the young couple. They'd mumbled short and insincere apologies for any inconvenience they'd caused, and then tramped in a line back over to the far side of the clearing, where this time the invisible door was evidently working again. Then the English couple had invited Eddie and Connie to accompany them back to the pier.

'So,' Connie said, after a while of standing looking down at the boat. 'Guess you're not from London, England after all.'

'Oh, no,' said the male one. He was wearing a white Gap T-shirt and khaki shorts, and had engaging green eyes. 'Well, not originally. Though we do have a small place in Islington at the moment. A *pied-à-terre*, really. Very convenient for the centre of town.'

'Where are you really from?' Eddie asked.

'Oh, quite some distance away. Miles and miles. I'm not sure you chaps have even found it yet.'

Connie swallowed. 'Do you look as gross in your dimension as Fran did?'

'Hardly,' the female one laughed. She had a neat blonde bob, and was slim and pretty. 'Actually we look exactly the same as we do here, but a couple of inches taller. No idea why.'

Eddie nodded. 'So what happens now?'

'Well, basically,' the male one said, glancing at his watch, 'we're all free to get on with our evenings. The invasion threat's been averted and, well, the night is yet young. Sorry to have involved you in so much trouble. Wished we'd known that Fran was the spy. Could have

sorted the whole thing out last night – though to be honest we were a little tipsy by the stage it all went off.'

'What are you?' Connie asked.

The woman shrugged. 'Police, angels, inspectors,' she said. 'Pick your metaphor. We sort things out. Though to be frank, at the moment what I mostly am is starving. It's probably about time for some dinner, isn't it, darling?'

'Absolutely,' the male one said. 'Now: the gatekeepers have been told not to mess around with this whole abduction nonsense any more, but of course they will. Incidentally, Eddie, you shouldn't really have been doing what you've been doing without a licence.'

'Well, you know how it is, out in the sticks,' Eddie said. 'We don't always do things by the book. But we generally get by.'

'Quite. Well . . .' The man dug around in his pocket, and pulled out a thin black piece of paper. 'Here's a licence. With our thanks.'

Eddie took it, turned it over. It had no writing on either side. 'This is it?'

'I'm afraid so. I suppose you could get it laminated if you wanted. One final favour: we're thinking of zipping up the coast tonight, Gulf side, maybe Sarasota and its environs, checking out some new restaurants. Any recommendations?'

'You could try Tommy Bahama's,' Eddie said, eyeing them carefully. 'That's pretty good.'

'What kind of food is it?'

'They specialise in a Floridian/Caribbean cuisine. Kind of a "Floribbean" thing, I guess you'd call it.'

The man frowned. 'Which is?'

'American. But with fruit in it.'

'Sounds perfect,' the woman beamed. 'Thanks awfully.'

The two aliens thanked Eddie and Connie once more, took each other's hands, and then vanished into thin air with a quiet pop.

Eddie and Connie stood in silence for quite a while.

Then Eddie coughed quietly. 'Sorry about Fran,' he said.

'She was a good waitress.'

'You didn't . . .'

'Actually, yes, we did, a couple of times. I'd rather not think about it right now.'

Eddie nodded for a while, and let quiet settle once more. Then: 'Can I buy you a beer?'

'Hell, no. I'll buy the beer. What you're buying me is food.'

'Crabby Dick's?'

'You read my mind.'

They climbed down into the boat, took a look back at the island before it disappeared, and then set off across the calm, flat water towards Key West and food and drink and the things we do so well. They figured they might as well make a night of it. It was only just after eight o'clock.

Couple of weeks later, Eddie was standing on the upper deck of the Havana Dock early one evening, bathed in soft peachy light and waiting for the sun to go down.

Even after seven months on the Key, he liked to watch it, and for the time being he liked living there too.

All around were couples and small groups, dressed smart casual for the evening, sitting in warm expectation and sipping at fruity drinks. Many were tourists, but there was a good sprinkling of locals, come to enjoy a thing of beauty because living with it hadn't staled them to its charm. There was a hum of loose chatter, but mainly it was quiet, largely because the female synth player was taking one of her all-too-infrequent breaks. Eddie hoped that by the time she came back, and discovered that someone had removed the fuses from each and every one of her keyboards, they would all have been able to watch the sunset in peace.

He was sipping his Margarita, which was punishingly strong because the woman who made them had a frightening crush on him and was also in his debt because he'd sorted out a problem she'd had involving the most psychotic of her many ex-husbands, when he saw a young woman walking up the way. She had long brown hair and was pretty, but her eyes were watchful and there was something in the set of her shoulders which said she wasn't here for the sunset but rather because she was worried and afraid and had heard in a bar there might be a man on the dock who could help do something about it.

Eddie lit a cigarette, and settled down to wait for her to find him.